THE BOXCAR CHILDREN
THE SPORTS SPECIAL

THE SOCCER MYSTERY
THE BASKETBALL MYSTERY
THE SPY IN THE BLEACHERS

created by
GERTRUDE CHANDLER WARNER

ALBERT WHITMAN & Company
Chicago, Illinois

The Boxcar Children Sports Special
created by Gertrude Chandler Warner.

ISBN: 978-0-8075-0889-3

10 9 8 7 6 5 4 3 2 LB 16 15 14 13 12

Cover art by Robert Papp.

For information about Albert Whitman & Company,
visit our web site at www.albertwhitman.com.

THE SOCCER MYSTERY

created by
GERTRUDE CHANDLER WARNER

Illustrated by Charles Tang

ALBERT WHITMAN & Company
Morton Grove, Illinois

ISBN 978-0-8075-7527-7

20 19 18 17 16 15 14 13 LB 15 14 13 12 11 10

Printed in the U.S.A.

Contents

CHAPTER 1

Let's Play Soccer

"Oh, Benny, what are you doing to Watch?" Violet Alden asked her six-year-old brother.

Benny Alden grinned. He had tied a bandanna around Watch's head with a leaf tucked under one side to make an eye patch. "I'm a pirate," he said. "And I am making Watch walk the plank."

Benny had put a board across the stump that the Aldens used as a step up into the old boxcar in their backyard. He was standing on top of the board. Watch, who was a small black-and-white dog, was standing at one end of the board.

"Okay, Watch, jump off the plank into the ocean!" Benny commanded.

Watch looked over his shoulder at Benny. Then he sat down on the end of the board and yawned.

Ten-year-old Violet laughed. "I don't think Watch wants to walk the plank."

"I know," said Benny. "I'm not a very good pirate yet. I need more practice." Benny had been very interested in pirates ever since he and his sisters, Violet and twelve-year-old Jessie, and his fourteen-year-old brother, Henry, had visited Charleston, South Carolina. They had gone to help a friend of their grandfather's rebuild her house after a hurricane. But they had ended up finding a pirate's treasure.

Benny jumped off the stump. Without his weight on it, the board tipped forward.

"Look out!" said Violet.

"Woof!" said Watch, and jumped onto the grass as the board fell off the stump.

Benny and Violet both laughed now.

Watch ran in circles around Benny, wagging his tail and looking pleased with himself.

"Come on," said Violet. "You'll have to practice being a pirate later. Soo Lee is here."

Soo Lee was the Aldens' cousin. She was the daughter of Aunt Alice and Uncle Joe. They lived in Greenfield, too.

Violet, Benny, and Watch went across the backyard toward the kitchen door of the big old white house where they lived.

The red boxcar was the Aldens' old home. The white house was their new one.

After their parents died, the Aldens had run away. They had heard that their grandfather was a mean person. They'd made a home in the abandoned boxcar in the woods, where they had found Watch and adopted him.

Then Grandfather Alden had found them, and he hadn't been mean at all. So the four Aldens and Watch had come to live with their grandfather in his house in Greenfield. And he had even moved the boxcar to the backyard so that they could visit it whenever they wanted.

"Maybe Soo Lee would like to play pirate," said Benny.

"No," said Violet. "Soo Lee is here so we can practice soccer. She brought her soccer ball. We signed up for the Greenfield Summer Soccer League, remember?"

"I remember," said Benny.

"The tryouts are this weekend," said Violet. "We want to be ready."

She opened the back door and they walked into the kitchen. Mrs. McGregor, the housekeeper, was stirring something in a big bowl.

"Is that a cake for dinner?" asked Benny hopefully.

"It might be," said Mrs. McGregor with a twinkle in her eye. "You'll find out later."

"We're going to practice soccer with Soo Lee," said Violet. "At the park. May we get anything for you while we are out?"

"Maybe ice cream to go with the cake?" added Benny.

Mrs. McGregor shook her head. "Thank

you, but I don't need anything. Not even ice cream. Don't be late for dinner, now."

"We won't!" Benny promised.

Soo Lee, Henry, and Jessie were in the front yard. They were kicking a soccer ball back and forth. When Soo Lee saw Benny and Violet, she put her foot on top of the ball and stopped it.

"Come on," she said. "Let's hurry and practice." She gave the ball to Jessie, who put it into her pack.

When they reached the park, Jessie took the ball out of her pack. Then Soo Lee took another ball out of her pack.

"Two balls!" said Violet. "But you only use one ball to play soccer, don't you?" Like Benny, Violet had never played soccer before.

"Don't worry. We'll just use two balls for practice," said Henry. He, Jessie, and Soo Lee had all played soccer before. Soo Lee was a very good soccer player. She had played in Korea, where she was born. Like her cousins, Soo Lee was an orphan. Aunt Alice and Uncle Joe had adopted her.

Soo Lee, Jessie, and Henry showed Benny and Violet how to kick. Then they showed them how to run and kick the ball to someone else to make a pass.

"You can use every part of your body to move the ball," Soo Lee explained. "Except your arms and hands. Only goalies can use their arms and hands to catch the ball and keep it from going in the goal."

Soo Lee, Henry, and Jessie showed Benny and Violet how to kick the ball and keep it just in front of their feet on the ground as they ran forward. "When you move the ball forward like that," Soo Lee explained, "it is called dribbling."

Then Soo Lee and Jessie put their backpacks next to each other a few feet apart. "This will be our goal," said Soo Lee. "I'll be the goalie. You divide into two teams and play against each other and try to score."

Henry and Violet were one team. Jessie and Benny were another. They kicked and passed the ball and tried to keep it away from each other and shoot it into the goal. But no one could score. Soo Lee caught every shot they kicked toward the goal.

Then Henry stood at the goal. He caught every shot, too.

"You're good at the goal. And you're tall. You would make a good goalie," Soo Lee told him. "Maybe you should try out for that."

Watch sat on the sidelines and watched them play. Sometimes he barked. Then, suddenly, just as Benny got the ball and tried to kick it toward the goal, Watch ran out onto the field! He knocked the ball away from Benny. Then Watch began to push the ball with his nose.

Everyone stopped, and when they did, Watch pushed the ball right past Henry and into the goal.

"Yeah, Watch!" cried Soo Lee.

"Watch is a good soccer player, too," said Violet. She wiped her forehead with her sleeve. "Whew! I'm tired."

"We should stop. We don't want to be too tired to practice tomorrow," said Jessie.

Everyone agreed that it was time to stop. But before they could go home, they had to chase Watch to get the soccer ball back. He was very good at keeping it away from the others.

At last Benny caught him. "Game's over, Watch," he said, laughing.

As they walked out of the park, Violet said, "Soccer is not as hard as I thought it would be."

"You are doing really well, Violet," said Soo Lee. "So are you, Benny."

"Thank you," said Benny. He bent down to pat Watch on the head. "But you know who the best player is? Watch!"

"Woof!" said Watch.

CHAPTER 2

Which Team Is the Best?

"Gosh," whispered Violet to Jessie. "Look at all these people! What if I'm not on a team with anyone I know?" Violet was a little shy, and sometimes meeting new people made her nervous.

Jessie said, "I'm glad there are a lot of people. That means we'll have lots of teams. We'll make new friends, too."

"Maybe," said Violet. She still felt shy. But Jessie's words had made her feel better.

The day for tryouts for the summer soccer league had come at last. The sun was shining, and the grass of the soccer fields next to the community center was very green. Everywhere, children of all ages were racing back and forth passing soccer balls to each other. Others were dribbling up and down the field.

"Look," said Benny. He pointed to a girl who was bouncing a ball on the top of her foot. As they watched, she bounced the ball higher and caught it with the top of her knee. Then she bounced it even higher and made it land on her head. She bounced the ball on her head a few times, then let it drop to the ground, where she caught it with her foot again.

The girl smiled a little as she played with the ball. Her dark ponytail swung behind her, brushing against her golden yellow shirt.

"Wow," said Violet. "That looks like magic."

Henry nodded. "It's called juggling. She looks as if she has very good soccer skills."

Just then a tall man wearing a cap with a picture of a soccer ball on it called, "Attention! Could I have your attention, please?"

Some of the people trying out for the soccer league came over to face the man. But others kept on playing. The man pushed his cap back and smoothed his short blond hair. Then he stepped up onto the bottom seat of the bleachers, raised a whistle to his lips, and blew it loudly.

All of the players stopped running and talking then, and gathered around him at the foot of the bleachers. "Thank you," he said briskly. "I'm Stan Post. Everyone can call me Stan. I'm the director of the Greenfield Community Center Summer Soccer League. I'll also be one of the coaches. Now, I'll introduce our other coaches and go over a few things before we begin tryouts."

A boy with long blond hair and a red shirt said loudly, "This is so boring! I know all the rules."

"I don't know all the rules," said Benny, frowning at the boy.

"Shhh!" said someone behind them.

The boy rolled his eyes, but he didn't say anything else.

When Stan had finished introducing the coaches, he had everyone write their name on a name tag and stick it to his or her shirt. Then he divided everybody into groups. He had each group dribble and pass and shoot while he and the coaches watched. Stan wrote lots of notes on a notepad he was carrying. So did some of the other coaches.

Then Stan divided the groups into smaller groups and each of the smaller groups went with a coach to different parts of the soccer field.

"We're going to watch everybody for a little bit longer to make sure we put you on the right teams," Stan explained.

Violet was relieved to see that Jessie was in her group. She was glad that she knew someone. But she was not so glad that the boy in the red shirt was also in her group.

"Okay, everyone," said the young woman who was their coach. "I'm Gillian McPhee.

Everyone calls me Gillian. We're going to practice a few more drills — moves and skills that you use to play soccer."

Violet said softly, "What if you don't know how to do a drill?"

Near her, the boy in the red shirt gave a huge exaggerated sigh of impatience. Violet felt her cheeks grow red.

But Gillian only smiled at Violet. "If you don't know a drill, I'll explain it to you," she said. She looked at Violet's name tag. "Just do your best, Violet. That's what is important."

Violet smiled back at Gillian, feeling less nervous. Gillian had friendly brown eyes. Her dark brown hair was short and curly, and she was wearing tiny earrings in the shape of soccer balls. She was rather tall and her legs looked strong.

The boy in the red shirt said, "What's important is winning. That's what my brother Stan said. He should know, since he is in charge of the league."

Gillian glanced over at the boy. "Winning is important, Robert," she said. "But so is having fun and trying hard." She raised her whistle to her lips. "Okay, everybody, let's go. We're going to practice passing."

At the other end of the field, Benny, Soo Lee, and Henry waited as the girl in the yellow shirt sprinted up to them. Their coach, Craig Crenshaw, was having them run relays. He ran up and down the sidelines with each group of sprinters, talking all the time.

"Good, good, good," they heard him pant as he ran past. "Keep going, that's it. Good, good, good." His wiry legs flew as he talked, and his sunburned face grew even redder while his wild reddish brown hair seemed to stand out like the mane of a lion around his head.

Soo Lee ran forward with the next group. The girl in the yellow shirt stopped and bent forward to rest her hands on her knees, trying to catch her breath.

"Wow, you're fast," said Benny.

The girl straightened up and fanned her face. "Thanks," she said cheerfully. She reached into her pocket and pulled something out. "I think this helps. Red licorice. Would you like some?"

"Yes, thank you. My name is Benny," said Benny, pointing to his name tag. He stared at the girl's name tag, not quite sure he could read the word.

"My name is Elena," she said. "Elena Perez." She broke some licorice off for herself and chewed it.

"You're a good player, too, aren't you?" asked Jessie. "We saw you juggling a little while ago."

"I practice a lot," Elena said. "Someday, I want to play for the Olympic soccer team."

"You will," said Benny thickly, chewing on a big piece of licorice. There was admiration in his voice.

"I hope so," said Elena. "I have been practicing for it for six years, ever since I was six years old."

"Six years old! That's how old I am," said Benny. "Maybe I can be an Olympic soccer player, too!"

"Maybe you can, Benny," said Jessie.

"But now it's your turn to run."

Benny looked up and saw that Henry had just gotten back. He took off running as fast as his legs could carry him.

A couple hours later, Stan stood up on the bottom bench of the bleachers and called everyone over.

"Thank you," he said. "You have all tried hard and played well. The coaches will meet and decide which players are on which team. We will post the results on the community center bulletin board tomorrow morning when the center opens. The teams will have their first practice then."

Stan, Craig, Gillian, and the other coaches walked back toward the community center. They talked and gestured as they walked.

"Whew!" said Jessie. "That was hard work!"

"But it was fun, too," said Violet.

"I like soccer," said Benny. "But it makes me hungry."

"Me, too," said Soo Lee.

Henry said, "I'm really thirsty. Let's go

get a drink of water from the water fountain inside. The water will be good and cold."

"Good idea," said Soo Lee. "Then I have to hurry home for dinner."

The community center was almost empty because it was late in the day. Each of the five children took long, cool drinks of water. They were about to leave when suddenly they heard loud voices coming from behind a partially open door just down the hall.

"I don't care what you say, Stan. It is important for everybody to get a chance to play," said a man's voice.

Jessie, Benny, and Soo Lee exchanged looks of surprise. They had heard that voice a lot that day. It was the voice of Craig Crenshaw.

A woman's voice said, "Yes. Craig is right. Everyone who tried out today should be on a team."

"Gillian," whispered Violet.

"Putting beginners in the league is a waste of time," said Stan's voice. "In case you've forgotten, Anthony Della, the head coach at the university, is looking for an assistant coach. And having a bunch of beginners playing for you is not the way to get the job."

"It's unfair not to include everybody. This is a community league — " Craig said. But before he could finish, Stan interrupted him.

"I don't care if it's fair or not. I'm not letting a bunch of beginners stand in my way!" snapped Stan. The door of the office flew open and he stalked out. He marched down the hall toward the door at the other end. He never even saw the children standing by the water fountain.

A moment of silence followed. Then someone inside the office sighed. "He's right, you know, Gillian. Coach Della will be looking for assistants who coach winners, not beginners."

The door of the office opened. Gillian and Craig came out. "I know," Gillian said. Then she saw the Aldens and stopped in surprise. "Oh! Hello!"

"Hi. We were just getting some water," said Jessie quickly. She didn't want the two coaches to think that they had been deliberately eavesdropping!

Gillian hesitated, then said, "That's good. It's important when you are hot and have been exercising to drink lots and lots of water."

She and Craig walked by and went out the front door.

The Aldens followed slowly. Outside, Soo Lee said, "Good-bye. I'll come over early tomorrow and we can go to the community center together to see which teams we are on."

"*If* we are put on a team," said Violet. "I don't think Stan wants beginners like Benny and me to play soccer."

Jessie said, "We will all be put on a team. Don't worry."

"I hope you're right, Jessie," said Henry.

CHAPTER 3

"You'll Be Sorry!"

"You're not eating very much breakfast, Benny," said Grandfather Alden the next morning.

"I'm not hungry," answered Benny. "I'm worried."

"Worried? About the results of the soccer tryouts?" asked his grandfather.

"Yes. I'm not that good at soccer yet," said Benny. "I need lots and lots of practice before I can be as good as Elena Perez."

"Elena Perez? I know Dr. Perez and her husband, but I've never met their daughter Elena," said Grandfather.

"Elena is a very good soccer player," said Jessie.

"Yes," said Violet. "She'll definitely be put on a team. But what if players who are beginners — like me — aren't put on a team?"

She was thinking of the conversation they had overheard among Gillian, Stan, and Craig. If Stan had his way, beginning players like Violet and Benny wouldn't be allowed to play at all.

"If you aren't put on a team, none of us will play in the league, either," said Henry.

Just then Mrs. McGregor came in with Soo Lee. When her cousins offered her breakfast, Soo Lee shook her head. "Hurry," she said. "It's almost time to go to the community center to see which soccer teams we are on."

The Aldens finished their breakfasts quickly. Benny drank all of his orange juice and finished his cereal, but he didn't ask for seconds as he usually did. Although he felt better knowing that his brother and sisters would help him, and would not play soccer without him, he was still a little worried.

When they got to the community center, they had to make their way through a large crowd of children who had gathered around the bulletin board by the front door.

Robert Post pushed past them as they reached the lists of teams. "Ha," he said to the boy who was with him. "I'm on the Bears. That's Stan's team and it's the best. I knew I'd be on it. We're going to win every game."

Violet's heart beat faster as she followed Henry, Jessie, and Soo Lee to the front of the crowd. She reached down and caught Benny's hand.

Benny reached out with his other hand and tugged on his older brother's shirt. "Am I on a team?" he asked.

Henry looked down with a big grin on his face. "You sure are," he said. "You and Violet are on the same team, the Panthers. Gillian is your coach."

"Yeah!" said Benny. He let go of Violet's hand and waved his arms in excitement.

"Oh, good," said Violet. She was very relieved, and very happy, too.

"I'm on your team also," said Elena to Violet. She came up behind the Aldens and pointed over Jessie's shoulder to her name on the list. "I was on Stan's team — the Bears — but I asked to be put on Gillian's team. I like Gillian."

The Aldens saw then that Elena's name had been on Stan's list, but had been crossed out.

Jessie said, "I'm on Craig's team, the Hawks. I like Craig. But I don't know anybody on my team."

"Henry and I are on the Bears, too," said Soo Lee. "With Robert." She didn't sound very happy about it. "And look, Henry, you're going to be one of the goalies. Robert is going to be the other."

"Okay, everybody," said Stan. "Time for practice. Let's go!" He raised his silver whistle and blew it loudly.

Although Violet and Benny were beginners, they weren't the only ones on Gillian's team who were just learning to play soccer.

Gillian divided the fifteen players on her team into three groups. She put experienced players in each group to help teach the beginners how to play.

"Good, Violet," said Gillian, when Violet kicked a pass right back to Elena.

Then she showed Benny how to run and kick the ball better. She was very patient and Violet and Benny soon understood why Elena had wanted to be on the team that Gillian was coaching. They were learning a lot and it was fun, too.

Jessie, who was standing at the front of two lines of players, kept glancing over at Violet and Benny and Elena. They were laughing together and seemed to be having such a good time!

"Okay, team," Craig said. "We're going to do a drill to practice getting to the ball first. You won't be able to get a goal if you let players on the other team get to the ball first."

He stood between the two lines of players and held the ball up. "When I throw the ball out in front of me, I want the player at the front of each line to run out and try to get to the ball first. The first player who gets to the ball, wins."

Craig threw the ball. But Jessie hadn't been listening. She'd been watching her brother and sister on Gillian's team.

"Jessie!" cried Craig, throwing up his hands. "What're you doing? You have to pay attention!"

"Sorry!" said Jessie, and ran out to try to get the ball. But the other player got there first.

"That's okay. We're going to practice this some more so you can try again," said Craig. "But you have to pay attention."

"I will," Jessie promised. She did better after that, but she still kept glancing over at the Panthers.

Henry and Soo Lee were paying attention to what they were doing on Stan's team, but they weren't having fun.

Stan talked all the time, just as Craig did. Unlike Craig, however, he didn't say very encouraging things.

"That's terrible!" Stan shouted at Soo

Lee when she kicked a ball at the goal and missed. "You'll never win if you make stupid mistakes like that! Next!"

Behind Soo Lee, Stan's younger brother Robert snickered. "That *was* bad," he said as he ran past Soo Lee. Then he kicked the ball he was dribbling right into the goal and right past Henry. He turned to Soo Lee with a smirk on his face. "That's the *right* way to do it," he told her.

Stan didn't seem to notice that his brother was being a bad sport. He just blew his whistle and said, "Next!"

Henry and Soo Lee tried hard and did their best. But no matter how good anyone on the Bears was or how hard a player worked, Stan never said anything nice. "Run faster!" he barked. "Kick the ball harder!"

"This is awful," Soo Lee whispered to Henry.

"I know," said Henry, glancing over toward the other teams. "No coach on any other team is yelling like Stan is."

Robert overheard Henry. "Those teams

are losers," he said. "Forget about them. We're going to be the winning team."

Henry and Soo Lee looked at each other. Each knew what the other was thinking. If they weren't having fun playing, winning didn't mean anything.

At the end of practice, Stan said, "That's it for now. You've got a lot of work to do. You Bears looked like a bunch of clumsy bear cubs out there today."

"Come on," Henry said to Soo Lee. "Let's go tell Stan we want to be put on another team." As the rest of their team walked off the field, Henry and Soo Lee walked up to Stan.

"We'd like to be put on another team, please," said Soo Lee.

Stan looked down at Soo Lee and frowned. "What are you talking about?"

"My cousin and I would like to be on another team."

"Why?" asked Stan, frowning harder. "The Bears are the best team, and you are good players. Why would you want to be on another team?"

"Because we aren't having any fun," said Henry boldly. "We want to play on a team that is fun to play on."

"Fun? *Fun?*" Stan said, as if he had never heard the word before. "You're not supposed to have fun. You're supposed to win!"

"We know. But we want to have fun, too," said Soo Lee.

Stan put his hands on his hips. "Fine," he snapped. He pointed toward Gillian's team. "Go play on her team if you are not interested in winning. But I'm warning you, you'll be sorry!"

CHAPTER 4

A Soccer Team Spy?

Soo Lee looked over her shoulder as they walked across the field toward Gillian. Stan was still standing where they had left him, glaring after them. "Uh-oh," she said to Henry in a low voice. "Stan looks really angry."

"Then I'm even more glad that we're not playing on his team anymore," said Henry.

Gillian's team had gathered around her. "Okay, everybody, you all did a good job. If we keep working hard and really trying, we're going to have a terrific soccer sum-

mer," Gillian said. "See you at the next practice."

As the soccer players left, Henry and Soo Lee walked up to Gillian to tell her that they were now on her team. "Great," said Gillian, writing their names down on her clipboard.

"Hooray," said Benny, giving a little skip.

"I'm glad," Violet said.

"I'm going to be on your team, too," said Jessie.

The others all looked over at her in surprise.

Jessie went on, "I like Craig. I think he's a good coach. But I want to play with you guys on the Panthers."

With a nod and smile, Gillian wrote Jessie's name on her clipboard list. "Welcome to the team," she said. "See you all at the next practice." She tucked her clipboard under her arm and walked back to the community center.

"Does anybody need a ride home?" asked Elena. She pointed toward a car in the parking lot. "My father's here to pick me up."

"I'd like a ride," Benny declared. "My legs are *tired!*"

"We're going to get ice cream," said Elena.

"And my stomach is *hungry*," added Benny.

Jessie ruffled her younger brother's hair. "You're always hungry, Benny. Especially for ice cream."

"I'd like some ice cream, too," said Violet.

"I guess we do want a ride," said Henry. "Thank you."

The six soccer players began to walk toward Mr. Perez's car. As they got closer to the parking lot at one side of the community center soccer fields, Jessie said, "Look over there, at the other end of the parking lot."

They all looked. They saw a battered blue van with a man sitting in it behind the steering wheel.

"Isn't he holding a pair of binoculars?" Jessie asked.

The others turned and looked at the van.

Henry squinted a little and said, "I think you're right, Jessie. He *is* holding binoculars. And he seems to have them turned in this direction. But why?"

"Maybe he is watching for birds," suggested Soo Lee.

"A soccer field is a funny place to bird-watch," said Elena. "If I were a bird, I wouldn't stay on a soccer field. You might get hit by a soccer ball!"

Just then the man in the van put down the binoculars, backed quickly out of the parking lot, and drove away.

"Why did he leave so suddenly?" Soo Lee wondered aloud.

"Maybe he's a spy!" exclaimed Benny.

Henry laughed. "Oh, Benny," he said. "I don't think so."

Elena introduced them to her father, and they drove to the ice-cream parlor. The six children all got ice-cream cones and went outside to sit at the tables on the sidewalk to eat them. The ice cream tasted good after the long, hot soccer practice.

"Soccer makes me hungry," said Benny.

He had gotten chocolate ice cream with chocolate sprinkles.

"Me, too," said Elena, who was eating a butterscotch sundae.

"I'm glad I'm on a team," said Violet. "I didn't think Stan was going to let beginners play."

"What are you talking about?" asked Elena. She looked very surprised.

The Aldens and Soo Lee told her about the conversation they had overheard the day before.

"Well, Gillian should get that coaching job," said Elena. "She's a great coach. She's definitely the best one for the job."

"Ha," said a familiar, sarcastic voice.

They all looked up to see Robert standing on the sidewalk in front of them. "Gillian's a crummy coach," said Robert. "Stan is the best coach." He looked at Henry and Soo Lee. "Too bad you quit the Bears. Now you won't get a chance to win any games."

"We will, too," said Soo Lee. "Gillian thinks we are a good team."

"She's just saying that," said Robert. "I bet she's really upset. Coaching a bunch of beginners is going to ruin her chances of getting that job. The university is only interested in coaches who can coach winning teams."

He turned and walked away.

For a moment no one spoke. Then Jessie said, "Wow. He might be a good soccer player, but he is definitely not a good person."

"Robert would be an even better player if he were a better sport," said Elena.

But Violet wasn't thinking about that. She looked around at the others. "Do you think it's true?" she said. "Do you think that if our team loses, Gillian won't have a chance of getting that coaching job?"

"I don't know, Violet," said Henry. "I don't know."

It was two weeks later and the last practice for all three teams before the first game. Robert caught a ball and kicked it hard out of the goal and down the field where the Bears were practicing. "Gotcha!" he shouted at the player who had kicked the ball.

"At least we don't have to play our first game against the Bears," said Soo Lee.

"Yes. It will be much more fun to play against the Silver City Rockets," agreed Jessie. The next day all three teams — the Bears, the Panthers, and the Hawks — were going to play against teams at the Silver City Community Center.

Stan had started his team's practice early and was already yelling at his players. Gillian had gone to the room where each team kept soccer balls and equipment.

Now she and Craig were coming back to start practices for their teams. Each was carrying a big net bag full of soccer balls.

Craig walked over to his team and Gillian came to join the Panthers. "Okay, everybody," she said. "Each of you take a soccer ball and jog around the field. Practice kicking the ball as you run."

She opened the bag and turned it upside down, and the soccer balls came spilling out.

But they didn't bounce everywhere as they usually did. They thudded to the ground and just lay there.

"What is this?" asked Gillian, bending over to pick up a soccer ball. She squeezed it between her hands and frowned. "This soccer ball is completely flat," she said.

"So is this one," said Elena, picking up another ball.

"And this one," cried Jessie.

"They're all flat," said Gillian.

At that moment, Craig came running over holding a soccer ball in his hands. "Look at this! *Look* at this!" he cried. "Every single ball, flat. No air. Like a pancake. This is no coincidence. Someone let the air out of my team's soccer balls."

"Mine, too," said Gillian. She looked around at the Panther team members. "Is this someone's idea of a joke? Did someone sneak into the equipment room and let the air out of the soccer balls?"

Everyone on the Panthers shook their heads.

"Well, whoever did it, it's not funny."

Gillian's normally pleasant expression was cross. "We're going to have to pump all these balls up before we can begin practice."

"No one on my team knows anything about it, either," said Craig. He raised his hand and waved vigorously. "There's Stan. Stan! Come over here, please."

"What's the problem?" asked Stan as he approached the two coaches.

"This is the problem," said Gillian. She showed Stan the balls, and she and Craig told him what had happened.

Stan didn't change expression as he listened. When Gillian and Craig were finished, he said, "I wonder how that happened," as if he weren't really interested.

Jessie stepped forward. "Who has a key to the equipment room?" she asked.

Stan raised one eyebrow. "I do. Craig and Gillian do. So does the director of the community center, of course. And the janitor."

"Five people," said Henry.

"I hope you're not implying that one of us would pull such a childish trick," Stan said.

"Someone did," Benny said.

"Well, it could have been anybody," said Stan. "I unlocked the equipment door when I got here, a little before practice was scheduled to begin. I usually do that, and I don't lock it back up until after practice is over." Stan checked his watch. "If you'll excuse me, I have a team to coach."

"But what about our teams' soccer balls?" protested Craig.

"There's a hand pump in the equipment room," said Stan, sounding bored. "I suggest you get started."

"He wasn't much help," said Craig.

"No. But we'd better get started pumping up those soccer balls," said Gillian.

Craig, Gillian, and some of the players on each team took turns pumping the balls up as fast as they could. But it still took a long time. When it was finished at last, Craig's team took the balls back to their field and began to practice.

Gillian gave each Panther a ball. Still looking cross, she said, "Let's get this started. With our first game tomorrow, we need every minute of practice we can get." She glanced toward the Bears, who were practicing on the next field, and her expression was unhappy.

The Panthers had worked hard. They were better players than they had been. But the Bears were better still.

"Who would let all the air out of the balls?" asked Elena as they ran and dribbled their soccer balls. "That was a mean thing to do."

"Robert's mean," said Benny. "Maybe he did it."

"You can't just say someone did something because they're mean," said Henry. "You have to have proof."

"Maybe we can find a witness," said Jessie.

"We'll look for clues after practice," said Henry.

"I know who might have done it," said Soo Lee suddenly. "Look. It's the same blue van that was here before."

The van was in the same place, on the far side of the parking lot. They could see someone in it, but they could not tell if the person was using binoculars.

"Wow," said Benny. "Do you think the spy did it?"

"I don't know," said Henry. "But we're going to find out, as soon as practice is over!"

After practice, however, the van was gone. And when they asked Gillian if she had seen anyone suspicious-looking loitering near the equipment room, she shook her head. "I've thought and thought about it," she said. "But I don't remember seeing anyone near it before practice. Except, of course, Craig. He was on his way to get his teams' practice balls and I ran into him."

"It sounds as if almost anybody could have gotten into the equipment room," said Henry.

"Yes," Gillian said. "But I'm going to talk to Stan about keeping the door locked from now on. We don't need any more pranks like this." She fished around in the pocket of her windbreaker and brought out her car keys. "See you at the game," she said.

The Aldens waved good-bye to Gillian and to Elena. "See you tomorrow in Silver City," Elena called out the car window as she drove away with her father.

Then they went to get their bikes, which they had left along one side of the soccer field.

Violet picked up her bike and was about to get on it when she stopped. "Look," she said, pointing. "The blue van is over there now!" She wasn't pointing across the parking lot. She was pointing toward the road that ran down the other side of the fields.

"Yes!" said Henry. "I think that's the same van."

"The spy," said Benny, getting excited.

"Not a spy," said Jessie. "But I think we should ride our bikes in that direction to see if he has binoculars this time."

Quickly the Aldens got on their bicycles and rode around the community center and down the sidewalk along the road where the van was parked.

Just as they pulled up next to the van, the driver turned and looked out the window.

He had on dark glasses and a blue-and-gold cap pulled low on his forehead.

When he saw the Aldens, he started the van and drove quickly away.

The Aldens tried to follow him, but the van was too fast. By the time they got to the corner, it had disappeared from sight.

"He doesn't want us to see him," said Henry as they pulled their bikes to a stop. "That's for sure."

"But who is he?" asked Jessie.

"And why is he watching us?" added Violet.

"He had binoculars this time, too," Soo Lee said. "I saw them on the dashboard."

"Well, even if he isn't a spy," said Benny, "it's a mystery, isn't it?"

"It is, Benny," agreed Jessie. "But this time, it's a mystery without any clues!"

CHAPTER 5

A Missing Soccer Player

"The Silver City Rockets look like a good soccer team," said Violet.

"Good. They will be fun to play against," said Jessie cheerfully. "And look. There's even a locker room where we can change into our new shirts."

All the soccer teams had gotten new shirts in their team colors, with the name of the team and a number on each shirt. The Panthers' colors were purple and white.

Jessie, Violet, and Soo Lee went into the locker room. They each put their packs into a locker. They took off their sneakers and put on their soccer cleats and their new shirts. Then they hurried out to join the other Panthers on the soccer field.

The two teams lined up on opposite ends of the field. Then the referee blew her whistle and the game began!

"Go, Panthers!" shouted Grandfather.

Not everybody could play at once. Only eleven players from each team were allowed on the field at any one time. Benny didn't start out playing the game. He stood on the sidelines with Jessie.

They cheered loudly whenever the Panthers got the ball. Gillian clapped and cheered, too. Then suddenly Elena got the ball. She ran as fast as she could with it, dodged around one of the Rockets, and kicked it into the goal!

"Yeah, Elena!" shouted Benny. He looked up at Dr. and Mr. Perez, who were also standing on the sidelines. "She's a great player," he told them. "I'm going to be a soccer player like Elena someday."

Dr. Perez laughed. "I know you will, Benny," she said.

Just then, Gillian came over. "Benny, I'm taking Violet out of the game so she can rest. I want you to go in and play in her place."

Benny ran out onto the field. Someone kicked the ball toward him. He raced toward it and kicked the ball as hard as he could — and tripped. The ball skidded away. A Rocket team member fell over Benny and the referee blew her whistle.

"Tripping," she said, pointing at Benny. "The other team gets to kick the ball."

"I didn't *mean* to trip her," said Benny. But he got on his feet and backed up while the Rocket player kicked the ball.

Benny hurried up and down the field as fast as his legs would carry him. Soon he was very tired. He was glad when Gillian took him out and put someone else in his place.

At halftime, the score was tied, 1–1. "We have ten minutes to rest," Gillian told the

Panthers. "Everybody get a drink of water from our cooler."

Elena said, "Coach, I've broken one of my shoelaces. I have an extra one in my pack in the locker room."

"You can go get it," Gillian told her. "But hurry. We don't have much time."

Elena trotted toward the locker room.

Soon the referee blew her whistle. "Time for the second half," she called.

Gillian looked around. "Elena's not back," she said.

"Time," said the referee again as the eleven Rocket players went out onto the field.

"Jessie, you go in for Elena," Gillian said.

The second half began. Now Henry was playing at the goal. The Rockets kicked the ball toward him, trying to get it past him. But he caught every one.

On the sidelines, Gillian looked around with a worried frown. "Elena's still not back," she said.

"I'll go look for her," Violet volunteered.

"Thank you," said Gillian.

Violet ran toward the locker room. She pushed the door, but it wouldn't move.

Violet pushed again. The door wouldn't budge. "Elena!" Violet called. "Elena!"

"I'm in here," called a muffled voice from the other side of the door. "Someone locked the door behind me and I couldn't get out. I've been calling and calling."

Violet heard people cheering from the soccer field. She glanced over her shoulder. The Rockets had scored.

Oh, no, she thought. *I have to get Elena out to help the team.* "Don't worry!" Violet said loudly. "I'll get you out."

She looked up and saw that a bolt high up on the door had been locked. She tried to reach it, but couldn't.

Quickly Violet looked around. She saw an empty metal trash can nearby. She hurried over to it, picked it up, and carried it back to the locker room door. Turning the trash can over, she stepped up onto the bottom of it.

Now she could reach the bolt. She pushed the bolt back, jumped off the trash

can, and called, "It's unlocked!"

Elena burst out of the locker room so fast that she knocked the trash can over. "Thanks," she gasped to Violet, and ran toward the soccer field.

After setting the trash can upright again, Violet followed Elena. As she reached the sidelines, she heard Elena explaining to Gillian what had happened.

Gillian's eyebrows drew together, but she didn't say anything. She just sent Elena into the game to play in someone else's place.

The Panthers played hard. So did the Rockets. In the end, the Rockets won, 2–1.

When the game was over, Gillian told the Panthers to go shake hands with the Rockets. The two teams shook hands and then went off the field.

"I should have caught that last ball," Henry said. "Then we would have at least tied."

"You couldn't help it," said Benny. "You slipped, just like I did."

Gillian held up her hands. "Everybody

played very well today. I'm proud of you. But we have a problem. Somebody locked Elena in the locker room at halftime. Does anybody know anything about this?"

All the Panther players were silent. Then someone said, "Maybe the janitor or someone else locked her in by mistake."

Shaking her head, Gillian said, "No. The janitor would know to leave the locker room unlocked during a game.

"Well, if this is somebody's idea of a joke, it is not funny," Gillian said. Then she said, "See you at practice, Panthers."

Grandfather Alden came up to join them. "All of you are doing very well," he said.

"Thank you," said Benny.

"Go get your things out of the locker room," Grandfather said, "and we'll go home for lunch. I think Mrs. McGregor is cooking a special lunch to celebrate your first soccer game."

"We didn't win," Jessie pointed out.

"Did you play your best?" asked Grandfather.

They all nodded.

"Then it's worth celebrating," he told them.

The Aldens headed for the locker rooms. Players from all the teams were going in and out of the doors of the two locker rooms as they finished their games and got ready to leave.

Robert brushed by them as they reached the community center. "Out of my way," he snapped. "I'm in a hurry. We're about to start our game."

Then he stopped. "Too bad you lost your game," he said to Henry and Soo Lee. "I told you that the Panthers were a losing team."

"How did you know we lost our game?" asked Soo Lee.

"I got here early and watched. I watched the Hawks, too," said Robert. "They got lucky and won. But they're still losers, too."

Jessie could feel herself getting angry at Robert, so she said, "Aren't you in a hurry? I think I heard the referee blow the whistle to start the game."

Robert spun around and sprinted toward the soccer field.

"Oh, Jessie. Did you really hear the referee blow her whistle?" asked Violet.

Jessie grinned. "Yes," she said. "But I think it was a whistle to start another game, not the one the Bears are in. I just didn't want to talk to Robert anymore, though, did you?"

"No!" declared Benny.

"Someone locked Elena in the locker room at halftime and someone let all the air out of our soccer balls," said Soo Lee. "Do you think the Panthers are a bad luck team?"

"No," said Jessie firmly. "We're not a bad luck team. But I think someone wants us to *think* we are."

Just then Violet grabbed Henry's arm. "Look," she whispered.

Henry and everyone else turned to look toward the front of the building. "What is it, Violet?" asked Henry in a puzzled voice. "I don't see anything."

"It's him," she said. "It's the man in the blue van!"

CHAPTER 6

Follow That Van!

"The blue van? You saw the blue van?" Jessie cried.

"No! No, I saw the man who was driving the blue van," said Violet. She hesitated. "At least, I think it was him. He was wearing dark glasses and a navy blue cap with gold trim pulled down low over his face."

Henry said, "It could be him. But where did he go?"

"We should look for him," said Jessie. "But we have to hurry. Grandfather is waiting."

"We'll divide up. Violet and I will check inside the building, Benny and Soo Lee can check the parking lot, and Jessie, you go see if he's at the soccer field. We'll meet back here in five minutes."

The Aldens and Soo Lee scattered to look for the mysterious man. Five minutes later they had reunited in front of the locker room doors.

"Not in the parking lot," said Soo Lee.

"But his blue van is!" added Benny.

"We didn't see him anywhere inside the building," Henry said.

"Where's Jessie?" Violet asked.

"Here I am," said Jessie, hurrying over. "And I found him!"

"Where?" asked Henry.

"Most of the people watching the games are standing on the sidelines," Jessie said. "But a few are sitting in the bleachers. He's sitting up at the very top of the bleachers, in the middle of a group of parents."

"Do you think he is somone's father?" asked Benny. "Can someone's father be a spy?"

Jessie shook her head. "I don't know, Benny. He wasn't talking to any of the other parents. And he wasn't cheering for anyone. He was just watching."

"I think we should watch him," said Henry. "Let's ask Grandfather if we can stay just a little while longer."

Mr. Alden agreed that they could stay. "But we have to leave at halftime," he said. "We don't want to be late for lunch."

The Aldens and Soo Lee decided to split up again to spy on the man in the navy blue cap. "If we go over there all together," said Jessie, "it might make him suspicious."

Henry and Soo Lee went to stand behind the bleachers. Violet, Benny, and Jessie took seats at the top, at the end away from the man in the navy hat. They took turns glancing in his direction to see what he was doing.

But he didn't do anything. He just watched the Bears playing soccer against the Eagles, the Silver City team. And sometimes he didn't seem to even be watching.

Sometimes he stared down at a notebook in his hand and wrote in it.

"Is he studying for something?" asked Violet.

"Maybe he's writing spy notes in invisible ink," said Benny. "Then he's going to leave the book, and another spy will come along and pick it up and get the notes."

But when halftime came, the man put the notebook into the pocket of his windbreaker and stood up. He glanced around, and Jessie, Violet, and Benny froze. For a long moment, it seemed as if his gaze rested on them, but it was hard to tell because he was wearing sunglasses.

Then he walked down the bleachers.

Jessie jumped up to follow him. But just then, the man turned and looked back up the bleachers.

Quickly Jessie pretended she was just stretching. She sat down again. "I don't think we can follow him," she said. "I think he is suspicious."

"What are we going to do?" asked Benny.

"Don't worry," said Violet. "Henry and Soo Lee will follow him."

They waited until the man was out of sight, then jumped up and hurried down the bleachers. Sure enough, they could see Henry and Soo Lee walking a short distance behind the man as he headed for the community center.

"Jessie, Benny, Violet," Grandfather called across the field to them. "It's time to go."

The three walked across the field to join their grandfather. "Where are Henry and Soo Lee?" he asked.

"Here they come," said Violet.

Henry and Soo Lee came up to join the others as they went to the parking lot.

"What happened?" asked Jessie.

Henry made a face. "Nothing," he said. "The man just got into the van and drove away."

"I think he was suspicious of us," said Jessie. "Maybe that's why he left."

"At least we know it is the same man with the van," Violet said.

"Yes," agreed Henry. "And if he was here this morning, he could have been the one who locked Elena in the locker room."

"He was at practice when all the air was let out of the soccer balls," said Violet.

"I think he is our best suspect," said Soo Lee.

"Right now," said Jessie, "he is our only suspect. But we can't prove anything until we find out why he would try to sabotage the Panthers."

It was after lunch, and the Aldens had gone out to visit their old boxcar in the backyard. Mrs. McGregor had made a very special lunch for them. Benny had had seconds of everything. He'd eaten so much lunch that it had made him sleepy, and now he was lying in the grass next to the boxcar, his eyes half closed. Watch was lying next to Benny with his head on Benny's chest. He was waiting for Benny to wake up and play. Soo Lee had gone home after lunch. She had been yawning, too, when she left.

"Are you taking a nap, Benny?" asked Violet.

"No," Benny answered. "I'm just resting my eyes."

Henry, who was sitting next to Violet in the doorway of the boxcar, grinned down at his younger brother.

"What are you doing, Jessie?" asked Violet, looking over her shoulder at her sister.

Sitting at the table inside the boxcar, Jessie had her chin propped on both fists. She was staring at the wall with narrowed eyes. At first she didn't answer her sister.

"Jessie?" said Violet. "Jessie?"

Jessie blinked and looked startled. "I'm sorry. I didn't hear you. I was thinking too hard, I guess."

"What were you thinking about?" asked Henry.

"Everything that has happened to the Panthers," said Jessie. "I was trying to figure out who did it and why."

She got up and came to join her brother and sister in the doorway of the boxcar. Violet moved over to one side to make room for Jessie in the middle.

"Someone let the air out of the soccer balls on the last practice before our game," said Jessie. "Then someone locked Elena in the locker room at the Silver City Community Center at halftime."

"Maybe one of the players on the Rockets did that," suggested Henry. "Elena is one of the best players on the Panthers. Maybe they thought it would help make us lose the game."

Jessie shook her head and said, "I thought about that. But no one on the Rockets could have let the air out of the soccer balls before practice. They would have had to know when and where we practiced, who our coach was, *and* come early, all the way from Silver City."

"That lets the Rockets out," agreed Henry.

"The best suspect is the stranger in the blue van," said Violet. "He was at practice and he was at the game. So he could have gotten to the soccer balls and followed Elena and locked her up."

Henry said, "True. But you know what, I don't think he's our only suspect."

"You mean Robert?" asked Jessie.

"No. I mean Stan," said Henry. "He would have a reason to make the Panthers lose. He wants to make sure everyone thinks the Bears are the best team and that he is the best coach, so he can get the coaching job at the university."

Violet said, "Craig and Gillian want that job, too. Maybe Craig did it to make Gillian look bad."

"But someone let the air out of the soccer balls for Craig's team, too," Jessie reminded her.

"Maybe Craig did it so he wouldn't be suspected," Henry said.

"Or Gillian could have done the same thing," Jessie said. She held up her fingers and counted off the suspects. "Stan, Gillian, Craig, and the stranger," she said. "Four suspects. And not enough clues."

"Do you think anything else will happen at soccer practice?" Violet asked.

"I do, Violet," said Henry. "Either at a practice or at a game. We'll have to be ready. We'll watch Stan, Craig, and Gillian very closely. Then maybe we can catch whoever is doing this."

CHAPTER 7

Pop Goes the Soccer Ball

"Catch it, Watch!" shouted Benny. He kicked the ball toward Watch. Watch ran after it and pushed it with his nose.

Watch, Benny, and Soo Lee were practicing soccer in front of the Aldens' house. They were playing keep-away, trying to keep Watch from getting the ball. But Watch was too fast for them. Every time Soo Lee or Benny kicked the ball, Watch ran like a flash toward it and knocked it out of the way with his nose. Then Soo Lee and Benny had to chase him to get it back.

Soo Lee kicked a ball up in the air. Watch circled under it and when it landed, he pounced.

Then, suddenly, there was a popping sound, followed by a hiss.

"Oh, no!" cried Soo Lee. "Watch bit the ball!"

"He was just trying to catch it," said Benny. The two of them ran toward Watch, and Watch ran away, carrying the ball in his teeth. They chased him all the way around the house before they caught him.

"Good boy, Watch," Benny panted. He sat down on the front steps with the ball. He squeezed the ball between his hands. More air hissed out.

"Let me see," said Soo Lee. She took the ball and examined it. "There," she said. "See. There are two teeth marks in the ball. Those are Watch's teeth marks."

"I'm sorry," said Benny. "But it was an accident."

"I know. It's okay," Soo Lee said. She reached down and petted Watch. "He was just practicing. He'll know next time not to bite the ball, won't you, Watch?"

"Woof," said Watch.

"We came out to play soccer with you," said Jessie. She, Violet, and Henry came out of the house and down the front steps.

Soo Lee held up the ball. "We can't. My soccer ball has a hole bitten in it."

She and Benny told the others what had happened.

Henry inspected Soo Lee's soccer ball. Then he said, "We should go to the Greenfield Sports Store and get you a new soccer ball, Soo Lee."

"Yes," said Jessie. "If we put all our money together, we can buy you a ball to replace the one Watch popped."

"You don't have to do that," said Soo Lee.

"Yes, we do," said Violet. "Besides, how can we practice soccer without a ball?"

"Okay," said Soo Lee.

Benny took Watch inside to stay with Mrs. McGregor. Then they all got on their bicycles and pedaled into Greenfield.

The Sports Store was on a corner near the park. They parked their bikes outside and went in.

"Watch would like this store a lot," said Benny. "It has all kinds of balls: soccer balls, baseballs, basketballs, even tennis balls and golf balls."

"Do you think he would bite holes in all of them?" asked Soo Lee. She and Benny burst out laughing.

Jessie smiled. "It's a good thing we didn't bring Watch!" she said.

"There's a ball like yours, Soo Lee," said Henry. He and Soo Lee picked up the ball and examined it.

"It is just the same as the other ball," Soo Lee agreed.

"Then that's the one we should get," said Jessie. The five children headed for the cash register. They had just paid for the ball and were about to leave the store when Soo Lee said, "Isn't that our coach? Isn't that Gillian over there?"

"It's Gillian *and* Stan," said Violet.

Gillian was standing next to a display of

soccer cleats. Facing her, Stan had a matching sweatshirt and pants with the price tags dangling off of them.

As they watched, Stan shook his head and raised one eyebrow.

Gillian put her hand on her hip and scowled.

"I don't think they are shopping together," said Violet softly. "It looks as if they are having a fight."

Stan shook his head again. Gillian raised her voice and suddenly they could hear her. "That's not why I'm complaining and you know it, Stan. I like the Panthers. They are a good team. But you kept almost all the best players for yourself. You've made it nearly impossible for anyone else in the league to have a chance of winning."

"You're the one who wanted to let players of every skill level play together," said Stan, raising his own voice.

"I have a good chance at that job as assistant coach with Coach Della at the university, as good a chance as you," said

Gillian angrily. "Or I *had* a good chance, until you did this."

Stan smiled. It wasn't a nice smile. He said, "If you're such a good coach, Gillian, you'll be able to make the Panthers into winners, won't you?"

"You won't get away with this, Stan," Gillian said angrily. "I promise you, I'm going to find a way to stop you." She turned and stormed down the aisle.

Stan stood and watched her leave, both eyebrows raised, the unpleasant smile still on his face. "May the best coach win," he said finally, and laughed nastily before turning and leaving the store.

"I thought Gillian liked being our coach!" cried Benny.

"She does, Benny. But she's right. Stan did keep most of the best players for himself. There's not a single beginner on his team," said Henry.

"She really wants that coaching job at the university," observed Soo Lee. "It sounds as if she would do almost anything to get it."

"Anything?" asked Jessie quickly.

"Possibly," said Henry. "Maybe even sabotage her own team to cover up that she is sabotaging other teams."

"The only other team that has had bad luck is Craig's," said Violet. "And I don't think Gillian is behind any of the things that have happened."

"I don't, either. And anyway, Stan's team is the one she's mad about. Why hasn't anything happened to Stan's team?" said Benny.

"That's a good question, Benny. I don't know," answered Jessie. The Aldens went outside and got on their bikes and pedaled slowly home. After getting a cool drink of lemonade from Mrs. McGregor, they went into the front yard to practice soccer. They practiced all the rest of the afternoon. Whenever they rested, they talked about the mystery.

By the end of the afternoon, they were all better soccer players. But they were no closer to solving the soccer mystery.

CHAPTER 8

A Fake Phone Call

"Hello?" said Violet, answering the phone. She listened for a moment and a worried expression crossed her face. "The game has been moved?" she asked. "Oh. Okay. Thank you." She hung up the phone.

The Aldens were at the breakfast table. Benny wasn't eating as big a breakfast as usual because the coach had told the team not to eat too much before a game. The Panthers were playing the Hawks that morning. But he wasn't nervous, the way he had been before his very first soccer game.

Everybody else was calmer, too. Henry drank his juice and began to eat a second piece of toast. Jessie finished her cereal and said to Violet, "The game has been moved?"

"Yes. We were supposed to play at the Greenfield Community Center, but it has been moved to Silver City," she told the others.

Just then Soo Lee came into the kitchen. "Hi, everybody," she said.

"Would you like some breakfast?" asked Mr. Alden.

Soo Lee wasn't as nervous as she had been before the first game, either. "Yes, please," she said. "I'd like some juice. There's plenty of time for me to have some today."

"Not if we have to go to Silver City to play," said Jessie.

"Silver City?" said Soo Lee, surprised. "But we're playing at the Greenfield Community Center."

"Someone just called and told Violet that the game has been moved," Benny said.

Looking even more surprised, Soo Lee said, "No one called and told me that."

"Maybe they called after you left," said Violet.

"And maybe Aunt Alice said you were coming here and would find out from us," added Benny.

"I guess so," said Soo Lee.

But Jessie was becoming suspicious. "Did the person who called tell you his name?" she asked Violet.

"Nooo," said Violet slowly. "It was a man's voice. But it was very deep, almost as if he were trying to disguise it. I didn't recognize it, and he didn't say who he was."

Jessie got up from the table and went to the telephone. She looked up Stan Post's name in the phone book and dialed his number.

"May I please speak to Stan Post?" she asked when someone answered.

"This is Stan Post," he said at the other end of the line.

"This is Jessie Alden. Has the game between the Panthers and the Hawks been moved?" she asked. She listened for a moment and nodded. "I didn't think so," she said.

She hung up the phone and turned to face the others. "The game hasn't been moved," she told them. "That phone call was a fake. Someone didn't want us to go to the game this morning!"

"Who would do a terrible thing like that?" gasped Violet.

"The same person who let the air out of the soccer balls and locked Elena in the dressing room," said Henry.

"If it was a man who called, it couldn't have been Gillian," said Benny.

"That's true, Benny," said Violet. "I didn't think she would do any of those mean things, anyway."

"Then maybe it was Craig," said Soo Lee.

"Or Stan," said Henry. "Did he sound surprised when you asked, Jessie?"

"No. He didn't even sound interested," said Jessie. She made a face.

"Don't forget the mysterious stranger," Violet said. "He could have found out who we are from anyone and called us."

Henry put down his fork. "Whoever it was, maybe we should get to the game a little early today."

Later that day, the Aldens were at the community center. The Panthers were ahead of the Hawks 1–0, but Henry didn't want the Hawks to score even one goal. Henry was the goalie.

He paced up and down in front of the goal. He watched the teams running up and down the field.

Suddenly one of the Hawks kicked the ball toward the goal. Jessie ran after the ball. So did the Hawk. Who would get there first?

The Hawk player beat Jessie. He kicked the ball again.

From the side of the field, Henry heard Benny shout, "Go, Henry! Go, Henry!"

Henry ran toward the ball. The Hawk player ran toward the ball.

This time Henry got there first. He fell on the ball and curled himself around it so that the Hawk player could not kick it again.

He heard cheers from his team and from the sidelines as he got up. Looking down, he realized he was covered with dirt and grass stains from falling. But he didn't care. He had caught the ball!

The referee blew her whistle. The game was over!

With the ball under one arm, Henry trotted toward the middle of the field. All the Panthers shook hands with all the Hawks. "Good game," they said to each other. Gillian and Craig had taught both teams to do that. It was part of being a good sport.

Then Henry walked off the field with Elena, Violet, and Jessie, smiling broadly.

"Good catch, Henry," said Elena.

"I sure am glad you were there to save that goal," Jessie said.

"I think it must be scary to be a goalie," said Violet. "I don't think I could run and catch the ball like that."

Benny and Soo Lee ran out to them. They had played in the first part of the game but had not been playing near the end.

"That was great, Henry," said Benny. "I'm going to be a goalie!"

"I thought you wanted to be a forward like Elena and score lots of goals," Soo Lee teased her cousin.

"I'm going to do both," declared Benny.

"I'm sure you will," said Grandfather Alden as he approached.

"Keep up the good work, Henry," said Gillian. "The whole team played wonderfully. I am very proud of you." She applauded the team. Then the team applauded her. After that, everyone began to get ready to leave.

Craig came over. He shook hands with Gillian. "Good game, Coach," he said.

"Thank you, Coach," she said. "Why don't we go get some breakfast? I was too nervous to eat this morning before the game."

"Did you hear that?" whispered Benny. "Our *coach* was nervous!"

"Good idea," said Craig. They smiled at each other. Then Craig said, "I'll give you a ride. Then we can come back here and watch more soccer."

The two coaches walked to Craig's car, got in, and drove away just as Stan and Robert pulled into the parking lot. Craig and Gillian waved. Stan nodded. Robert stared straight ahead, ignoring them.

"He's being a bad sport, Grandfather," Benny said.

"He certainly is," said Grandfather.

"I'm learning a lot about soccer," Benny went on happily.

Grandfather Alden smiled and patted Benny's arm. "You all are," he said.

Just then Jessie, who had been staring across the parking lot, said, "I don't believe it! The blue van is here."

"Is the stranger in it?" asked Soo Lee. "Does he have binoculars?"

"I don't see anyone in the van," said

Jessie. She looked around. "I don't see the stranger anywhere."

The others looked all around, too. They didn't see him, either.

Grandfather Alden said, "The Perezes and I are going to go sit in the bleachers to watch the Bears play the Silver City Rockets."

"We'll come sit with you," said Henry. "But not right away."

Their grandfather's eyes twinkled. He knew that they were working on a mystery. But he only said, "Okay. See you soon."

As Mr. Alden and the Perezes walked away, Violet said, "If no one is around the blue van, maybe this would be a good time to go look inside. We might find some clues."

"Good idea, Violet," said Henry.

"Wait until Robert and Stan leave the parking lot," Soo Lee warned.

"Maybe we can look in Stan's car, too," said Jessie.

After the Post brothers had left the parking lot, the Aldens strolled over to the van.

They kept a sharp watch for the stranger, but they didn't see him anywhere.

At last they reached the van. Henry looked over his shoulder. "No one is in the parking lot," he said. "No one has even noticed we're here."

"Good," said Jessie. She led the way around to the other side of the van, so that no one could see them.

Looking inside, they could see that the van was neat and clean. A pair of binoculars was on the seat.

"Look," said Soo Lee. She pointed to a small sticker in the lower right-hand corner of the windshield.

"It's blue and gold," said Benny. "U . . . N . . . I . . . What does it say?"

"University," said Soo Lee. "It's a parking sticker for the university."

"Athletic Staff," read Henry, leaning over to examine the parking sticker, too. "See? Athletic Staff Number one-two-three-four-five-seven."

"Does the spy work for the university?" asked Benny.

"I don't think he's a spy, Benny," said Violet.

Suddenly Jessie said, "Someone's coming."

"Hide," said Henry. "Everybody duck down!"

They crouched low, so they couldn't be seen near the van. Nobody moved.

Was it the stranger? Had he seen them at his van and come back? Was he about to catch them?

CHAPTER 9

Trapped!

Footsteps crossed the parking lot. For a moment it seemed as if they were heading toward the van. Then, nearby, the children heard a car door open.

It stayed open for what seemed like a very long time. Then the car door shut and the footsteps moved away, back across the parking lot and out toward the soccer field.

Jessie let out a long, slow sigh of relief. She stood up so she could see through the van's window.

Robert was walking back toward the soccer field carrying his gear bag.

"Whew," said Henry. "It's a good thing we weren't looking in Stan's car. Robert must have forgotten his gear bag."

"Yes. And he would have caught us for sure," said Jessie.

"Maybe we should go," suggested Violet nervously. "There aren't any clues here."

The Aldens looked around the parking lot. But no one was there. In the distance, they could see Robert walking toward his team, still holding his gear bag.

The Aldens left the parking lot as fast as they could without running. They had just reached the far end of the soccer field where the Bears were going to play the Rockets, when Soo Lee said, "There he is."

They all stopped and stared. The stranger was walking toward them. As he passed Robert, Robert spoke to the stranger.

The stranger stopped. He didn't look pleased for a moment. Then he gave Robert a small smile and nodded.

"Look at that!" Violet gasped. "*Robert* is

smiling! And it's a nice smile. I've never seen him do that!"

"I don't think anybody has," said Henry.

The stranger walked on. He came straight toward the Aldens. They kept walking, too.

He barely glanced at them as he walked by. But Robert stayed where he was a moment longer, staring after the stranger. Then he turned and went to join his team.

"Wow," breathed Jessie. "That really *was* a close call. If we had stayed much longer, the stranger would definitely have caught us."

"Does Robert know him?" asked Benny. "Is Robert working with the spy? Is Robert a spy, too?"

"It's a possibility, Benny," said Henry. "But I still don't know why. It doesn't make sense."

The Bears were standing on the sidelines. Robert straightened up as the Aldens and Soo Lee passed. Robert reached into his bag and pulled out his goalie gloves. He began putting them on.

Suddenly he stopped. "Oh, no!" he said.

In spite of himself, Henry stopped. "What's wrong?"

"I don't believe this!" said Robert in a loud voice. "Someone smeared peanut butter all over my goalie gloves. They're ruined!"

"Peanut butter on your gloves?" said Benny. He wrinkled his nose. "Yuk."

Stan came over. "What's wrong here?"

Robert showed his brother the gloves.

"When did this happen?" Stan demanded.

"It must have happened when I left my gear bag in the car," said Robert. "It's the only time it's been out of my sight. Someone was watching, and they went to the car and sabotaged my gloves."

"Do you have another pair?" asked Stan.

"No," said Robert. "I — "

"Get a pair," said Stan.

"But I — "

"I don't want to hear excuses. The game is about to begin. Just do it," Stan snapped, and walked away.

"I have a pair of gloves you can borrow," said Henry.

Robert swung around to face them. He drew back his upper lip. "Oh, yeah?" he said, with a sneer in his voice. Then he looked past Henry. "You do?" he said, in a much nicer tone. "Would you mind if I used them? I'd really appreciate it."

"Sure," said Henry. He unzipped his own gear bag and took out his gloves. He handed them to Robert.

Robert smiled. It was another nice, normal, friendly smile. "Thanks, Henry," he said. "Thanks a lot."

He put the gloves on and ran out on the field to the goal.

"Why did Robert get so friendly all of a sudden?" wondered Soo Lee aloud.

"You did a good thing," Benny told Henry. "You were a good sport."

Henry laughed. "It's a lot more fun than being a bad sport. Come on, let's go sit with Grandfather." The Aldens headed up to the bleachers.

A gust of wind whipped across the field.

A familiar blue-and-gold cap suddenly whisked by Jessie's foot. She reached down and grabbed it. She turned and froze.

The stranger was standing right behind them. He was holding his binoculars in one hand. He held out his other hand to Jessie. "You caught my cap," he said. "Thank you."

"Y-you're welcome," said Jessie. She handed the man his cap, then turned and hurried after the others.

As they sat down, Jessie watched the stranger out of the corner of her eye. He climbed to the top corner of the bleachers and sat down. He pulled his cap down and raised his binoculars to his eyes.

She nudged Henry. "There he is," she said. "He was right behind us when you gave your gloves to Robert. I think he went to the van to get his binoculars."

"Hmmm," said Henry.

Violet said in a puzzled voice, "Who would sneak out to the parking lot and put peanut butter on Robert's gloves? It couldn't have been Benny's spy, could it have?"

"You're right, Violet, it couldn't have been," said Soo Lee. "We went into the parking lot just as Robert and Stan left it. And we were there the whole time, even when Robert came back to get his gear bag."

"Well, if the spy didn't do it, that means he didn't do any of those other bad things, right?" asked Benny.

Jessie's thoughts were whirling. "I don't know," she said. She put one hand on her forehead and tried to figure it out. She concentrated with all her might.

She lowered her hand and looked over at the stranger. Then she repeated, "I don't know who's done the bad things. But I think I do know how we can find out who your spy is, Benny!"

The man behind the counter was stuffing envelopes.

"Excuse me," said Jessie.

The man looked at Jessie over the tops of his glasses. "Yes?" he said.

"We'd like some information, please," said Jessie.

The Aldens had ridden their bikes over to the university. It had been a long ride, and they were very tired. Soo Lee hadn't been able to come with them.

"What sort of information?" asked the man.

"We'd like to find out who a car registration number belongs to," said Henry.

"Number one-two-three-four-five-seven," chimed in Benny proudly. "It's like counting, except that the last number is wrong."

The man got up from his desk and crossed the room to a file cabinet. He opened a drawer and rifled through some files. Finally he said, "Yes, we have a vehicle registered at the university under that number."

"Who is it?" asked Violet.

The man swung around and peered at Violet now. "Why do you want to know?" he asked. "Has there been an accident?"

"Not exactly," said Jessie. "I don't think the things that have been happening have been accidents."

The man peered at them all for a moment longer. Then he said, "I'm not supposed to give out that information without proper authorization."

"What?" said Benny.

"He can't tell us," said Henry.

"No," said the man. "I can't. Not without permission."

"How can we get permission?" asked Jessie.

"From the office manager," said the man. He added, "She's not in today. She'll be back tomorrow."

"Tomorrow!" cried Benny. "That's too long."

"That's the best I can do," said the man.

The Aldens walked slowly out of the office. They were very discouraged. They walked down the front steps of the building and across the campus to the bike rack where they had parked their bikes.

The university had big stone buildings,

smooth green lawns, and majestic oak trees lining the sidewalks. But the Aldens didn't notice.

"That's not fair," said Benny.

"We could ride our bikes back over tomorrow," said Violet.

"I guess that's what we'll have to do," said Jessie.

"No," said Henry. "We won't."

They all looked at him in amazement.

"Why not?" asked Violet.

"If the blue van is here," said Henry, "it is parked in the Athletic Center parking lot. Remember? It was an athletic staff parking sticker."

"You're right," said Jessie, getting excited. "And even if it is not there, maybe we can ask people who work there and they will know who the blue van belongs to."

"Yes!" cried Henry.

"Oh, good," said Violet as the Aldens got on their bikes and began to pedal to the Athletic Center. "I'm glad we don't have to ride our bikes all the way back here tomorrow."

As they reached the parking lot for the Athletic Center, Jessie slowed her bike to a halt. The others pulled up behind her.

Benny pointed. "There it is," he said. "There's the blue van."

"Yes, it is," said Henry. "And we're not going to have to ask anyone who it belongs to."

"Why not?" asked Benny.

"Because the parking place it is in has someone's name on it," Violet explained, staring.

"Who? Who is it?" cried Benny.

"Anthony Della," said Jessie. Then she read aloud the sign on the parking place where the blue van sat: "Reserved Parking. Coach Anthony Della."

Although it was a long ride home from the university, the Aldens didn't feel tired. They had too much to think about. When they finally did get home, they got a pitcher of lemonade from Mrs. McGregor and took it out to the boxcar. They sat on the grass next to the boxcar, with the pitcher on the stump, and talked about the mystery.

"Coach Della couldn't have done all those things," said Violet.

"No, he couldn't have," said Henry. "He has no reason to."

Benny picked up a stick and threw it for Watch. "Then why is Coach Della spying on us?" he asked.

"He's not spying on *us*, Benny," said Jessie. "But you're right, he is a spy."

Benny's eyes widened. "He is?" he asked.

With a laugh, Jessie said, "Not a bad spy, Benny. But remember? He is hiring a new assistant coach at the university."

"And Stan, Gillian, and Craig have all applied for the job," said Henry. "So Coach Della has been coming to watch them coach. But he didn't want them to know he was watching, so he has been careful not to be seen or recognized."

"But if Coach Della didn't do it, and Gillian didn't do it, who did? Craig?"

"Craig couldn't have been the one who put peanut butter on Robert's gloves," said

Henry. "Don't forget, Craig and Gillian had already left when Robert got there."

"And Robert said that the only time his gear bag was out of his sight was when he left it in the car," said Violet.

"But wait a minute," said Jessie. "No one came into the parking lot after Robert and Stan left Stan's car. We were there and we would have seen them. No one came near Stan's car except . . ."

"Robert!" said Henry.

"Robert? Robert is mean, but why would he do all those bad things?" asked Benny. "And why would he put peanut butter on his own gloves?"

"So no one would suspect him," said Violet.

Henry said, "But we've figured it out. And I think I know how we can trap him!"

"How?" asked Jessie eagerly.

"Like this," said Henry. "Listen . . ."

CHAPTER 10

A Soccer Trap

"Outstanding practice, everyone," said Gillian. "We're in good shape for the game with the Bears tomorrow afternoon. Go home and get some rest now."

Gillian slid her coach's clipboard into her gear bag, slung her bag over her shoulder, and walked to her car.

Henry picked up his own bag and walked over to Robert, who was standing on the sidelines of the next soccer field with his team. Soo Lee and the other Aldens followed.

"Did you get new gloves for the game?" asked Henry. Robert looked up and frowned.

"Yes," he said. "So if you were hoping I wouldn't, forget it. I'm going to catch every shot the Panthers try to kick into the goal."

"It's going to be an interesting game," said Henry. "I'm looking forward to it."

"Ha," said Robert.

Jessie said to Soo Lee in a loud voice, "You know what? I bet Gillian is looking forward to tomorrow morning even more than tomorrow afternoon."

"Why?" asked Soo Lee.

"Didn't you hear the good news?" Violet said. "Gillian has an interview for the coaching job at the university tomorrow morning."

"At eight o'clock," Benny burst out. "She's leaving at seven A.M. just to make sure she gets there on time."

"That's great," said Soo Lee.

Henry glanced over at Robert. "Good luck tomorrow," he said to Robert pleasantly.

"I'm not the one who's going to need it," said Robert. "The Panthers will. Especially your coach!" He turned and marched away.

"I think Robert believed us," said Violet softly.

"I think so, too," said Benny.

"We'll find out," said Jessie. "Tomorrow morning."

Watch yawned. "Shhh," said Benny. Then Benny yawned, too.

Henry looked at his watch. "It's almost seven A.M.," he whispered to Jessie.

"What if he doesn't come?" Jessie whispered back.

Violet said very, very softly, "I hear someone!"

The Aldens crouched lower behind the hedge along one side of Gillian's driveway. On the other side of the hedge, Gillian's car was parked in the driveway. They could see it by peering through the branches of the hedge.

As they watched, a figure on a bicycle

rode down the sidewalk toward them. The bicycle slowed down. Then it stopped.

Robert Post got off. He parked his bike on the sidewalk and walked slowly up the driveway. Once he stopped and looked all around, as if he suspected a trap.

No one moved a muscle. At last Robert started walking again. He reached the car and crouched down next to it.

"What is he doing?" whispered Violet.

Just then, they heard a hissing sound. Benny knew that sound. He had heard it when Watch had accidentally bitten a hole in the soccer ball. "He's letting the air out of her tires!" Benny cried, forgetting to keep his voice down.

Robert jumped to his feet. He looked wildly around. Then he sprinted toward his bicycle.

The Aldens ran after him. "Stop!" Henry cried.

Robert grabbed his bicycle. Watch ran past them all. He jumped at the bicycle and it fell over with a loud crash. Robert fell, too.

He looked up. The Aldens and Soo Lee had him surrounded.

"Your dog pushed me down," he said. "You're going to get in a lot of trouble for that."

"No, we're not," said Jessie. "You are the one who is in trouble."

"I — I don't know what you are talking about," said Robert.

"Yes, you do!" shouted Benny.

"You're the one who's been sabotaging the teams," said Violet.

"You let the air out of the balls. You locked Elena in the locker room," said Soo Lee.

"And you tried to make us think that our game had been changed," said Jessie.

"Why would I do that?" protested Robert. "Besides, someone tried to sabotage me! Someone put peanut butter on my goalie gloves."

"No. You did that. So no one would suspect you," said Henry. "You were the only one to go near your car when you'd left your gear bag in it. We know because we were in the parking lot and we saw you."

"Oh," said Robert. He sounded very much like a soccer ball that had the air let out of it.

"But why?" asked Violet. "Why did you do it?"

Robert pushed his bicycle to one side and got up slowly. He said, "I was trying to help my brother."

"How would doing all those things help your brother?" asked Soo Lee. "The Bears were winning anyway."

"I know. But I wanted to make sure he won. Stan's the best. I wanted it to look as if Craig and Gillian, especially Gillian, were careless and disorganized," said Robert. "I borrowed the key from Stan's key chain and slipped into the storage room one afternoon when no one was around to let the air out of the soccer balls."

"And you locked Elena in the locker room," said Benny.

"I hadn't planned on that," said Robert. "But I saw her going in as I was coming out of the boys' locker room, so I just locked the door behind her. It was so easy!"

"You called us, too, and disguised your voice and told us our game had been moved," said Violet.

"Yes," said Robert. "And when I heard that Gillian was going for an interview, I knew I had to stop her. But that wasn't true, was it? It was a trap, to catch me."

"You only did those things when Coach Della was around," said Henry. "Even that time when I lent you my goalie gloves and you were polite to me — it was only because Coach Della was standing right behind me."

"You know about Coach Della? Yes. I saw him and recognized him right away. But I didn't tell anyone. I decided this would be a good chance to make sure Stan got the job at the university. And I thought the only way for him to get the job was to make sure his team won every game. Winning is everything," said Robert. "That's what Stan says."

"It's not true," said Benny. "You were cheating and being a bad sport. And when you do that, you don't win."

Robert looked around at the five Aldens. "What are you going to do?"

"Call the police!" said Benny.

"No, Benny. We're not going to call the police. But, Robert, you have to tell Stan what you did. If you don't, we will. It was wrong," said Jessie.

"I know," said Robert. He picked up his bike. As the Aldens watched, he got on it and pedaled slowly away.

"We caught him," crowed Benny. "Didn't we, Watch?"

Watch barked happily. Then Benny yawned. "We caught him," he said. "And now I'm sleepy."

"Me, too," said Henry. "Let's go home and get some rest. We've got an important game this afternoon!"

"Go, go, go," shouted Grandfather Alden.

"Woof, woof, woof," barked Watch, wagging his tail and pulling at his leash.

Out on the soccer field, Benny, Violet,

Jessie, and Soo Lee played as hard as they could. At the goal, Henry tried to catch every ball.

"Good! Good! You guys are doing a great job!" Gillian shouted.

"Run harder! You can do better than that!" Stan shouted at his team.

Henry jumped for a ball. It hit the tips of his fingers and went into the goal.

The Panther fans groaned. But Gillian called, "That's okay! Keep trying."

Elena got the ball and ran down the field. She passed it to Jessie. Jessie passed it to Violet. Violet kicked it back to Elena. Elena kicked the ball into the goal.

Now the score was tied 1–1.

But the game was almost over. Everyone played harder than ever. Suddenly a Bear player ran down the field with the ball and kicked it into the goal, just past Henry's outstretched arms.

The score was 2–1. And that was how the game ended.

"We won, we won, we won!" chanted the Bears.

Although they were disappointed that they had lost, the Panthers went out to the middle of the field to shake hands. Some of the Bears ignored them. But Robert led the others over to the Panthers. He shook hands with all the Aldens and Soo Lee. "Good game," he said.

As the Panthers walked off the field, Coach Della came up to Gillian. "Congratulations on a game well played," he said. This time, Coach Della wasn't wearing dark glasses and a hat pulled over his eyes.

"Coach Della!" said Gillian. "I didn't know you were here."

"I've been around," said Coach Della with a little smile. "And when you get a moment, I've got a job offer I'd like to discuss with you."

Gillian stood very still. Her cheeks got pink. "A job offer?" she said.

"Yes. I like your style. You aren't afraid to take challenges, and believe me, I know what a challenge it is to have a team with so many skill levels, from beginners to experienced players."

"Thank you," said Gillian, sounding stunned. "We didn't win very many games, though."

Coach Della smiled more broadly. "Winning isn't the only thing — although it *is* important. Come to my office tomorrow morning at nine and we'll work out the details."

"I'll be there," promised Gillian.

Coach Della nodded and walked back across the field.

"Hooray!" shouted Henry. "Hooray for Gillian!"

"Yes. You are a *real* winner," said Jessie.

"When I grow up," said Benny, "I'm going to go to the university and play soccer for you, Gillian."

"Me, too," said Elena.

"Me, too," said Violet.

Then the Panthers gave their coach a victory cheer. It had been a winning season after all.

"Hurry," urged Benny. "Or someone will get our seats."

He jumped out of the car and pointed toward the university stadium.

"It's okay, Benny," said Violet, catching Benny's hand. "The tickets Gillian gave us are special seats. No one else can sit in them."

"Are you sure?" asked Benny.

"Yes," said Grandfather Alden with a laugh. "We're sure."

"Hello," someone called.

The Aldens turned.

"It's Stan and Robert," said Soo Lee.

Sure enough, the brothers were walking across the stadium parking lot toward them.

"What are you doing here?" Jessie asked.

Stan said, "We came to watch the university's first soccer game of the new season. I'm glad we ran into you. Robert and I both have something to say to you." Stan put his hand on his younger brother's shoulder.

Clearing his throat, Robert said, "I'm sorry about what I did. It was wrong. And you were right, it was cheating and being a bad sport."

"And I was wrong, too," said Stan.

"Robert learned his win-at-all-costs attitude from me. I didn't realize how bad I had gotten until this happened. And until I lost that coaching job."

Henry held out his hand. He and Robert shook hands. Then all the Aldens shook hands with Robert and Stan.

"The game will be starting soon. We'd better get into the stadium," said Grandfather.

"Just one other thing," said Stan. "Craig got a job coaching at the university, too."

"Oh, I'm glad," said Jessie. "He's a good coach."

"And," Stan went on, "I've been asked to organize the Greenfield Community Center Summer Soccer League again next summer. It's going to be a league for everyone — all players. I want to make sure you'll join."

"Yes!" said Benny.

"Thank you," said Jessie. "We'll be there."

Then they all hurried into the stadium.

"There's Gillian!" said Violet as they sat down.

"Do you think she's nervous?" asked Soo Lee.

"I'm sure she is," said Henry. "But that's okay. She'll do a good job anyway."

"I'm still nervous before a soccer game," said Benny to his grandfather. "But it's not as bad. I'm getting better all the time. When I go to the university to play soccer for Gillian, I'll hardly be nervous at all."

The players went out onto the field. The referee blew the whistle and the game began.

Benny leaned over to his grandfather. "And don't worry," he told him. "If you don't understand anything about the game, just ask me!"

THE BASKETBALL MYSTERY

created by
GERTRUDE CHANDLER WARNER

Illustrated by Charles Tang

ALBERT WHITMAN & Company
Morton Grove, Illinois

ISBN 978-0-8075-0576-2

10 9 LB 15 14 13 12 11 10

Printed in the U.S.A.

Contents

CHAPTER 1

Turnovers and Twins

"Over here! Pass it to me!" Benny Alden yelled, waving his arms. He and his sister Violet just needed one more basket to break the tie.

Violet looked over at Benny. She looked down at Soo Lee. Her five-year-old cousin was right beside her. Violet was quick. With both hands, she passed the ball to Benny.

Soo Lee scooted after it. Too late! Benny caught the ball. He took aim and arched it into the basket!

"Eight to ten. You won!" Benny's older

brother, Henry, yelled from across the driveway. "Soo Lee and I will get you next time."

The Aldens' backyard basketball game
was over. The children plopped down on
the cool grass next to twelve-year-old Jessie
Alden, who had sat out this game. Their
dog, Watch, waited for someone to roll him
the ball. He liked basketball, too!

"Henry's the basketball champ in high
school," Benny said, "but we're the champs
in Grandfather's driveway. I like our new
basketball stand. It's not too tall. The net
over the garage is for big kids. But this one
is just right for me and Soo Lee."

"You two are going to catch up to the rest
of us in no time," Jessie said. "Then watch
out, everybody!" She pushed the basketball
across the grass with her foot. Watch chased
after it. He pushed the ball back to Jessie
with his nose. She rolled it to him again.

"Soo Lee was just like a little shadow
guarding me," Violet told everyone.

"Speaking of shadows, look at that."
Henry pointed to a long shadow moving up
the sunny driveway.

Watch saw the shadow, too. He let the basketball roll down the driveway. He ran after the shadow instead.

The Aldens heard the fast, pleasant thump of a basketball hitting the driveway. Then, swoosh! The ball sailed right into the big net over the garage.

"Who threw that?" Jessie asked.

The children looked down the driveway. The sun was in their eyes. All they saw were two skinny shadows crisscrossing each other.

The Aldens heard a young woman's voice. "That's okay, Watch. We're friends."

Watch yipped and yapped and ran in circles. He liked these people with the long shadows.

The Aldens scrambled up from the grass. The two strangers dribbled and ran and jumped. They shot baskets from up close, from down the driveway, from behind their backs. They didn't miss a single shot.

The Aldens looked at one another. Who were these basketball wizards?

The children heard the screen door bang.

Grandfather Alden stood on the back porch. He smiled at the young woman and the young man. Both of them were tall, brown-haired, and fast on their feet.

"Do you know them, Grandfather?" Benny asked. "They just showed up and started shooting baskets in our yard."

Mr. Alden broke into a big smile. "You know the surprise guests that Mrs. McGregor's been baking for? Well, here they are!"

The young man and woman stopped playing. They shook hands with Mr. Alden.

"Sorry, Mr. Alden. We got carried away when we saw the basketball roll down your driveway," the young woman said. "Buzz and I just had to try it out after being cooped up in our car."

"Come meet our mystery guests," Mr. Alden said to the children. "Buzz, Tipper, these are my grandchildren. Let's start with Henry, who's fourteen. This one is Jessie, who's twelve. That's Violet, our ten-year-old. All three of them play basketball on our neighborhood teams."

"What about us?" Soo Lee asked.

Mr. Alden patted the little Korean girl's head. "Why, of course, I would never leave you out, Soo Lee. This is Cousin Joe and Cousin Alice's daughter. And last but not least, here's Benny. He's six now. He and Soo Lee are catching up to my older grandchildren in basketball. I just bought them that junior-size stand to practice with. Children, meet Buzz and Tipper Nettleton."

Henry's eyes opened wide. "Are you the famous Nettleton twins?"

The young woman laughed. "Sometimes we're the not-so-famous Nettleton twins, too!"

"Wow!" Henry shook the twins' hands. "I've seen your names all over our Hall of Fame board at school. My high school coach sometimes plays old tapes of your championship basketball games."

"My coach does, too." Jessie held her hand out to Tipper Nettleton. "She said ever since you played for Greenfield High, lots more girls sign up for basketball. Congratulations on winning the Most Valuable Player trophy. Nobody from Greenfield ever won it before."

Tipper smiled. "Thanks. Buzz and I both love basketball. It's a great game —"

"Enough basketball talk," the young man said, interrupting his sister. "I'd better get our luggage, Tip."

Now the Aldens noticed another shadow. This one seemed to pass over Tipper Nettleton's smiling face.

"Sorry, did I say something wrong?" Jessie asked after Buzz and Grandfather Alden left. "It's true, though. You really are the most famous basketball player from Greenfield."

Tipper put her finger to her lips. "Sometimes it's better not to talk too much about that. Up until I won the MVP trophy last month, Buzz and I have always been proud of each other. But I think he's getting a little tired of hearing about my award."

The Aldens were surprised to hear this. They were always happy when someone in their family won something. But they were polite children and didn't say another word.

Everyone headed out front to help Buzz and Mr. Alden with the luggage.

Benny and Soo Lee picked up Buzz's big sports bag.

"That's the name of your college, right?" Benny asked when he saw the bright orange letters on the bag. "I can read."

"And I can carry heavy things," Soo Lee said. She and Benny each lifted one end of the sports bag. "Benny and I help the teams."

Buzz cheered up a little when he heard this. "Well, Tipper and I could use a couple of good helpers. We came to coach some of the neighborhood teams. That's one of the reasons your grandfather invited us to visit."

Henry lifted a suitcase from the trunk. "I heard you two were coming to Greenfield, but I didn't know you'd be staying with us! Maybe you can give us some good basketball tips."

Buzz finally started smiling again. "That's why we're here."

Grandfather closed the trunk. "Buzz and

Tipper are too modest. They've also offered to play in a fund-raising game for the new sports center on the center's Opening Day. And there's one last surprise. Should I tell them, Tipper?"

Benny and Soo Lee tugged Mr. Alden's sleeve. "Another surprise?"

Mr. Alden had a hard time keeping secrets from his grandchildren. "Tipper is donating her Most Valuable Player trophy to the new sports center. The mayor will be coming and perhaps television people as well. Now, what do you children think of that?"

"Neat!" Jessie said. "We'll have a big basketball day in Greenfield."

Soo Lee put down her end of the sports bag. She looked up at Tipper. "This is heavy. Is your trophy in here?"

Before Tipper could answer, Buzz picked up the bag. "This is *my* bag. If you want to help Tipper, you can carry her bag instead."

Benny and Soo Lee didn't know what to say. They weren't used to cross words. They watched Buzz head up the porch stairs with his sports bag and suitcase.

Tipper spoke to the children softly. "You know what? I'll show you my trophy some other time. Buzz is . . . uh . . . tired after our long drive."

The children led Tipper into the big white house where they now lived with their grandfather. Awhile back, after their parents had died, the children had lived in a boxcar in the woods. After Grandfather found them there, he brought them home to his house, with its comfy beds and delicious meals. As a surprise, he had brought the boxcar home. Now it was a playhouse in the backyard.

"Welcome," a white-haired woman called out cheerily when she saw Tipper. "I'm Mrs. McGregor, the Aldens' housekeeper. When I first met you and Buzz, you were just two little babies in a carriage. Mr. Alden told me that your father and grandfather were famous Greenfield players, too. I guess it runs in the family."

"So does being tall." Tipper ducked her head under the kitchen doorway so she wouldn't bang her forehead.

"Well, you must be hungry after your long drive to Greenfield. Come try some of my apple turnovers. I've been hiding them from Benny," Mrs. McGregor said with a wink. "I just sent your brother upstairs. He said he needed a rest. I told him to take the front guest room. I made up the guest bed for you in Jessie's bedroom."

Tipper heard a door bang upstairs. "Thank you so much, Mrs. McGregor. That will be fine. Buzz is tired from our trip."

"Are you tired?" Mr. Alden asked. "We can hold off on Mrs. McGregor's treats until you rest up."

Tipper pulled out a chair. She stretched her long legs under the kitchen table. "I'm more hungry than tired. Apple turnovers are one of my favorite things."

"I know what turnovers are," Benny announced. "They're something to eat. And know what else? There are turnovers in basketball, too, but not the kind you eat!"

Tipper's face brightened when she heard this. "Good for you, Benny! A basketball turnover happens after a player makes a mistake and the other team gets the ball."

"An apple turnover happens after Mrs. McGregor bakes," Benny said. "Then the turnovers go to us!"

Everyone laughed at Benny's joke.

Mr. Alden raised his coffee cup. "Here's to Tipper Nettleton, the Most Valuable Player in the country."

The children clinked their milk glasses against Tipper's glass and Mr. Alden's cup.

Everyone was quiet as they ate. They heard Buzz's footsteps in the guest room overhead.

Benny brushed some crumbs from his lips. "Mmm. Buzz is sure missing something good."

Tipper put down her glass. "Buzz has been missing a lot of good things lately. Every time someone mentions my trophy, he makes an excuse to get away."

This surprised Henry. "I thought twins never got jealous of each other."

Tipper smiled a little. "Buzz and I never had a smidgen of jealousy between us until now. After all, Buzz plays men's basketball, and I play on a women's team. Buzz has always been my biggest fan, and I'm his."

"So why isn't Buzz happy for you now?" Jessie wanted to know.

Tipper went on, "My trophy seems to be the problem. Winning it made me happy, but it was hard for Buzz."

Mr. Alden stirred his coffee and turned to Tipper. "Ah, yes. Your grandfather mentioned that you hope to study medicine after college. I understand Buzz plans to continue playing basketball. I suppose the Most Valuable Player trophy would have helped him more than it will help you."

Tipper stared down at her plate. "Exactly. That's why I'm donating it to the sports center. Buzz won't have to see it around all the time."

"There, there," Mrs. McGregor said kindly. "Finish your turnover. You'll feel better. You don't know these children. Why, they'll make Buzz forget all about that trophy."

Suddenly Tipper pushed back her chair. "The trophy! I didn't see anyone bring it in.

Besides being valuable to me, it's worth a lot of money. It's made out of silver."

The Aldens followed Tipper out to the car. Tipper unlocked the trunk. "It's not here! I thought Buzz put it behind the suitcases. Wait, I'd better ask him about it."

Tipper was gone in a flash. A couple of minutes later, she was back. "He said it's in the backseat."

Benny and Soo Lee went around to the side of the car.

"There's something shiny on the floor!" Benny yelled. "See?"

Tipper looked through the car window. "Whew! That's it. I'll unlock the door."

But Tipper didn't have to unlock anything. When she pulled the handle, the door opened right away. "I can't believe Buzz didn't lock the car. Thank goodness no one saw the trophy. If it were missing, it would spoil all the plans for the dedication of the sports center. I'm going to put this in a safe place. I don't want anything to happen to it before I give it to the sports center on Opening Day."

CHAPTER 2

Something Borrowed

Tha-thump! Tha-thump! Tha-thump!

"What's going on?" Jessie asked when she heard Watch at her bedroom window early the next morning.

Watch had stuck his head under the window shade to see what was making the noise outside. All Jessie could see were his hind legs and his tail wagging back and forth.

When the thumping stopped, Jessie heard voices.

"Okay, Henry, just use your fingertips to control the ball while you run."

"Basketball?" Jessie said, stretching out. "So early in the morning?"

She looked across the room. Tipper had already made up the guest bed and gone downstairs, Jessie guessed.

Watch pulled at Jessie's covers.

"I know. I know," Jessie said. "You want to be out playing basketball, too."

In no time, Jessie was dressed in shorts and sneakers. Watch raced ahead to the kitchen. Mrs. McGregor was sliding a muffin tin from the oven. The kitchen table was set for company.

"Oh, I forgot," Jessie said. "Those basketball people are coming over to meet with Tipper and Buzz."

Jessie looked out the kitchen window. Tipper was giving Benny, Soo Lee, and Violet some basketball lessons. Buzz was still helping Henry.

Mr. Alden came into the kitchen for his morning cup of coffee. "No sleeping in today, right, Jessie? Looks as if the Nettletons have started an Alden Basketball Clinic in our own backyard."

Mrs. McGregor set the warm muffins on a plate. "Benny and Soo Lee asked Buzz for lessons first thing this morning. Benny thought that would cheer up Buzz. And you know what? Benny was right. All that young man needed was a good night's sleep and some Aldens begging for his attention."

"He won't have to worry about getting our attention!" Jessie said on her way out back. "I'm going out for some basketball lessons, too."

Jessie wasn't the only Greenfield player who hoped to get some coaching from the talented twins. Word of their arrival had spread fast. Within half an hour, several neighborhood children appeared in the Aldens' backyard.

"You're so lucky," Patsy Cutter said when Jessie came out. "Imagine, Tipper Nettleton staying right in your own house!"

Patsy Cutter was a new friend Jessie and Violet had made. She was the best player on their team, the Fast Breakers, but she didn't have many friends.

"How come you didn't tell me about Tipper after practice the other day?" Patsy asked. "Are you and Violet keeping her to yourselves?"

"Grandfather didn't even tell us the twins were staying with us," Violet explained.

"Come on!" Patsy answered. "You just didn't want anybody to know."

When Tipper overheard this, she came over to the girls. She gave Patsy a big smile. "It's true. Mr. Alden wanted to surprise his grandchildren. Buzz and I were the surprise! I hope we live up to it."

Patsy just stared up at Tipper in amazement.

Finally Jessie spoke up. "Tipper, this is our friend — and teammate — Patsy Cutter. She's the best player on the Fast Breakers. Patsy, meet Tipper Nettleton."

Patsy's face grew red. "I . . . I can't . . . I can't believe I'm actually meeting you. I watch all your college games on television so I can play like you."

"Well, if you want, I can show you a few things now," Tipper said cheerfully. "You, too, Violet and Jessie."

"Go ahead, Tipper. It's okay to give Patsy a private lesson," Jessie joked. "We don't want to keep you all to ourselves."

"I hope Tipper teaches her about sharing the ball," Violet whispered. "Patsy never passes the ball to me. "It must be because I'm the youngest one on our team."

Jessie curled the end of her ponytail around her finger. She looked on as Tipper coached Patsy. "It's not just you, Violet. Patsy sometimes forgets she's on a team. Maybe Tipper will teach her more about passing the ball to other players instead of just making baskets herself."

A few minutes later, everyone looked up when three tall people walked down the driveway.

"It's Mr. Fowler, one of the referees who helps out with the teams," Jessie said. "Oh, and our coach is with him. I didn't know they were the basketball people coming over. I wonder who the other person is."

When Tipper saw the three visitors, she stared at the tall young woman in the group. Finally she stepped a little closer. "Hi, I'm . . . Oh, my goodness. I don't believe it! You're Courtney Post, right? Amazing! Are you one of the coaches for the neighborhood teams, too?"

The Aldens looked on, puzzled. How did Tipper Nettleton know their coach?

"Yes, I am," the young woman answered without a smile. "I guess we'll meet on the same side of the court for a change."

Buzz gave Tipper a gentle arm punch. "What do you know? You two old rivals meet again. But this time it's friendly, not like when Greenfield High played Warwick. Hi, Courtney, I'm Buzz — the other Nettleton twin."

Courtney ignored Tipper and turned to Buzz. "Hi, Buzz. I guess they didn't tell Tipper that she'll be helping me coach the Fast Breakers."

"Listen, I couldn't be happier, Courtney. Honest," Tipper said. "I always admired your playing so much, even though I feared it! Nobody made me lose more sleep over games than you. I hope we'll be friends."

Again Courtney ignored Tipper. What was going on? the Aldens wondered.

Courtney introduced the other people with her. "Frank, Tom, come meet the great basketball legend Buzz Nettleton. Buzz, this is Frank Fowler. He referees some of the games. As for Tom, he coaches the Rockets, one of the neighborhood teams. When he's not doing that, he works as a painter at the sports center. He's finishing up the paint job before it officially opens."

Buzz shook both men's hands. "Hey, I know you — Tom Hooper! Didn't you play for Warwick a couple of years before my class at Greenfield High? And Frank, I know I've heard your name."

Before Buzz could continue, Frank Fowler said quickly, "No need to go into details. Now that we've all met, let's sit down and get our plans organized. The kids in Greenfield are the big basketball stars now, not us."

"Yoo-hoo," Mrs. McGregor called out

from the kitchen window. "There's coffee and muffins in here. You can bring in your paperwork and work around the kitchen table. Everything's all set."

After the grown-ups went inside, Patsy Cutter began shooting baskets again. "Tipper just showed me a couple of new moves. Look how great I'm getting already!" she yelled as she made basket after basket.

Everyone else waited for Patsy to share the ball. But she never did. Finally the other players gave up.

"I'll get us some juice," Henry told everyone. "After that, let's have a half-court game."

Henry went inside to fetch juice and cups from the kitchen. He noticed everyone seemed awfully quiet around the table.

"Gee, you'd think they were talking about insurance or something boring — not basketball," Henry told the other children when he returned. "If I were famous players like them, I'd be going over all the great old games. They don't seem to care for one another much."

"Not like us, right, Henry?" Soo Lee grinned at her cousin.

"No, not like us," Henry agreed. "I hope Grandfather doesn't notice that they're not too friendly. He donated a lot of money to the sports center so people would have fun together."

Henry poured out juice for everyone. "My coach at school told me that when Buzz was a senior at Greenfield High, he broke Frank Fowler's record for the most points ever made. Maybe Mr. Fowler is still upset about that."

"That was such a long time ago," Jessie said. "He's a lot older than Buzz. Why would he still care?"

Patsy put her juice cup down on the grass. "Players always care about being the best. If I had the record, I would never, ever want anybody to break it. Oops, look what I just did." Patsy's paper cup had tipped over, spilling juice on her shorts.

"You can go to the upstairs bathroom and wash them off in cold water," Jessie said. "I have lots of shorts in the bottom drawer of

my dresser. Go ahead and borrow a pair. My room is next to the bathroom."

"Hurry back," Henry called out to Patsy. "We have enough kids here for a quick game."

After Patsy left, Henry organized the older children into two teams. "Benny and Soo Lee, you can keep score and be the referees. Whoever gets to ten points first wins."

Benny and Soo Lee took their jobs very seriously.

"Foul!" Benny shouted when a boy named James brushed by Jessie.

Soo Lee counted the score with some pebbles. The game was short and ended ten minutes later.

That's when Jessie noticed Patsy hadn't returned. "I wonder what happened to her. I'll go check."

Jessie scooted through the kitchen. She overheard Frank Fowler talking in a cross voice. "No, I disagree, Buzz. You haven't lived in Greenfield for a long time. It's not a good idea to team up kids from the south end with north end players. No way."

"Fine. Whatever you say, Frank," Buzz answered quietly. "Now, how about having Tom make up the practice schedules?"

Frank Fowler disagreed with this suggestion, too. "No, I have a computer at home, and Tom doesn't."

Jessie overheard Tom's nervous laugh. "Give me a paintbrush or a basketball any day. I'm not too good with computers and writing things down. It's okay by me if Frank handles the paperwork."

"Good. That's settled," Jessie heard Frank Fowler say.

Jessie headed upstairs. She checked the bathroom. Patsy's shorts were hanging on a towel bar in the shower. But Patsy didn't seem to be around. Maybe she had gone home without telling anyone. Jessie stopped by her room to get a stopwatch for Benny and Soo Lee.

When Jessie stepped inside, she jumped back. "Patsy! You scared me," Jessie said when she saw her friend standing next to Tipper's bed. "Oh, good, you found some shorts. I thought you went home."

Something heavy dropped to the floor.

"What was that?" asked Jessie.

Patsy looked worried. "I was, uh . . . looking at these pictures on this bookcase, that's all. A big book fell down. I'll pick it up."

"Fine," Jessie said. She went over to her desk for the stopwatch. She caught Patsy's reflection in the mirror. Whatever Patsy picked up didn't seem to be a book.

"Come on, let's go out," Jessie told Patsy. "Everybody's waiting for us."

CHAPTER 3

A Big Mix-up

Poor Mrs. McGregor. For the next few days she cooked up a storm for Buzz and Tipper. But the busy twins were hardly ever home!

"Goodness, those two are going to turn into skeletons," Mrs. McGregor told the children. "What they need is good home cooking, not all these banquets and such that they have to attend."

"Now, now, Mrs. McGregor," Mr. Alden said. "None of your delicious leftovers will go to waste in this house."

Benny patted his stomach. "See, I'm not turning into a skeleton."

Mr. Alden laughed. "Everybody in Greenfield wants to meet the twins before they start coaching the neighborhood teams. The newspaper is full of pictures of them visiting schools and youth groups. And they're going to be on television. I hope they don't wear themselves out."

Violet had been quiet all through dinner. Now she spoke up. "I hope Tipper has enough time for the Fast Breakers tonight. I need help on my passing. Courtney spends nearly all her time with Patsy. She's already a good player."

Jessie turned to her sister. "Patsy does take up a lot of the coach's time. Look, tonight is our first practice with Tipper coaching. I know she'll give everyone lots of attention. She wants to make the Fast Breakers into a super team."

"How are your Blazers doing, Henry?" Mr. Alden asked.

Henry seemed a little quiet. "Well, Grandfather, I can hardly wait for Buzz to start coaching my team. Then Mr. Fowler can go back to being the referee. He's been coaching, and for some reason he doesn't seem to like me."

"Frank is a hard one to figure out, isn't he?" Mr. Alden said. "When we were organizing the sports center, he was one of our biggest boosters. He had all kinds of plans."

"I know," Henry broke in. "Wasn't it his idea to have a fund-raising game with all the best players who graduated from all the high schools around Greenfield?"

"Indeed, it was his excellent idea," Mr. Alden said. "That's why I arranged for the twins to come back to Greenfield for a visit. Something changed with Frank after he heard about that."

Henry nodded. "Everybody thinks Mr. Fowler is upset that Buzz broke his high school record. Whenever anyone mentions Buzz, Mr. Fowler changes the subject. Anyway, things should get better starting tomorrow."

"Why is that, Henry?" Violet asked.

Henry studied a piece of paper. "Buzz left

me a copy of his coaching schedule. He's due to practice with the Blazers tomorrow afternoon. Mr. Fowler will be away at a conference for most of the day. We won't have to worry about Buzz getting in his way."

The children helped clear the dinner table.

"Well, I hope Courtney and Tipper get along at our practice tonight," Jessie said, handing Henry the dishes. "After all, they were on opposite teams when they were in high school."

"They're not too friendly, either," Henry said as he loaded the dishwasher. "But at least Tipper didn't break Courtney's high school record."

An hour later, Mr. Alden drove Jessie and Violet to the new sports center. The building wasn't quite finished yet, but the indoor and outdoor basketball courts were ready for practice. The Fast Breakers girls were the first to use the indoor court.

"There's the twins' car," Violet said when

Mr. Alden pulled up. "That means they're back from the banquet. We're a few minutes early. Maybe Tipper can help me before the rest of the team gets here."

"See you later, Grandfather," Jessie said. "The twins are going to drive us home at nine o'clock."

The Greenfield Sports Center had a nice new smell of fresh paint and wood. Jessie and Violet stopped to look at the display case in the lobby.

" '*James Alden, Donor.*' That's Grandfather's name!" Violet said. "Now everyone who wants to play basketball can come here."

Jessie and Violet headed toward the gym. Their feet slapped against the new tile floors. Every sound echoed through the empty halls.

A minute later the girls heard angry words echoing through the halls as well.

"Somebody's having an argument," Jessie said.

The girls slowed down. Should they go in the gym? Or make a lot of noise so the people would hear them and stop arguing?

"It's easy for you to come in and take over for a couple weeks," a young woman said. "But I'm the one who's still going to be here after you leave Greenfield."

The halls were quiet. Jessie and Violet wondered what to do next.

"I'm sorry," the second person said. "I didn't want to force my ideas on the girls. I just thought —"

"Everybody knows what you think from all those interviews you do. But that doesn't mean I have to agree with everything you say. I still think we should pick out the best players and give them the most training. Then they can lead the team."

"That's Courtney's voice," Jessie whispered. "She and Tipper are having a disagreement."

Violet nodded. "Let's make a lot of noise so they'll hear us."

Jessie coughed. She and Violet took heavy steps. They didn't want to break in on the two young women during an argument.

Courtney and Tipper turned around when the Aldens walked in. Tipper looked flushed and upset. Courtney fiddled with some papers.

"Hi," Jessie said. "I guess we're early for practice. We saw your car outside, Tipper, so we just came in. Is Buzz here?"

Tipper cleared her throat. "He wanted to try the outdoor court now that the spotlights are hooked up. Then he has some errands to run. He'll be back to pick us up at nine. I wonder if I should go outside and practice, too. I don't seem to be much help around here."

Before the Aldens could say anything, some of the other Fast Breakers girls arrived. Courtney's and Tipper's cross words were soon forgotten. The girls squealed with excitement. Tipper Nettleton was really here!

One of the girls quickly removed a sneaker. She handed it to Tipper. "Hi, I'm Amy Billings," the girl said. "I know this might seem funny, but would you autograph my sneaker?"

Tipper laughed. "Sure thing, Amy." She picked up a pen from the coaches' table. "It's not the first time I've autographed a sneaker or somebody's hand or even a napkin in a restaurant. Here you go."

Pretty soon all the girls wanted their sneakers autographed. Suddenly everyone heard the scream of a whistle.

"Listen up, people!" Courtney yelled over the girls' voices. "Are we here to play basketball or get autographs? Anybody who isn't ready for practice shouldn't be here."

The girls' voices died down. They put their sneakers back on. Courtney blew the whistle again. The girls knew what this meant. No more talking. Make a circle. Listen to the coach. After all, they were the Fast Breakers. They wanted their team to be the best.

"Okay, we're going to do some drills tonight," Courtney told the players. "Tipper will take some girls. I'll take the others."

Several of the girls whispered when they heard this. All the girls wanted to be in Tipper's group.

But Courtney Post had other plans. "Okay," she began. "I want the following girls to line up here next to me: Patsy, Jessie, Mary Kate, and Ellen. Everyone else stand next to Tipper."

The girls stood in two rows side by side. Courtney and Tipper checked their clipboards to decide which drills to cover.

"What's the matter, Violet?" Jessie whispered when she saw how disappointed her sister looked. "Do you mind that we're not in the same group?"

Violet shook her head. "It's not that. Courtney just likes a few players best. She teaches them to keep the ball to themselves. I know you wouldn't do that. But the others she picked just hold on to the ball, especially Patsy. The rest of us won't get to play very much."

Jessie gave Violet's hand a squeeze. "Tipper won't let that happen. No way. Besides, now that she's coaching your group, you'll get so good, you'll be on the court all the time."

Courtney blew her whistle again. "Okay,

girls. Here's what's happening. Tipper will get some basketballs from the storage room. Everybody else, meet with your groups down at each end of the court. Ready?"

"May I have the key to the storage room?" Tipper asked Courtney.

Courtney stared at Tipper. "I gave you the key already. Don't you remember? Right after that newspaper interview here yesterday morning?"

Tipper's face turned red. "I'm sorry. I've been so busy, I guess I forgot. It's probably in my gym bag or my purse. I'll go check."

After Tipper left, Courtney spoke to the girls. "Well, it's too bad we have to waste so much time waiting around. We should be playing. But that's what happens when you're famous."

When Tipper returned, she was empty-handed. "I'm sorry, Courtney. I couldn't find the key. Are you sure you gave it to me? There were so many people around yesterday morning, I just don't remember."

Courtney shifted from one foot to the other. She checked her watch. "It's already seven-thirty. We haven't got time for this. There's a basketball in my gym bag. We really need a bunch of them, but one will have to do. I'll use it for my group. Did you bring one?"

"No, but Buzz did!" Tipper said, relieved. "He's practicing on the outdoor court — that is, if he's still there. I'll borrow his basketball. Wait up, girls!" she called out to her group.

A few minutes later, Tipper returned empty-handed again. "Buzz left. I don't think he'll be back until nine o'clock to pick us up." She look nervously at Courtney. "Do you think our group could share your basketball?"

Courtney rolled her eyes. She took a long time to answer. "I guess so. But you'll have to wait until we're done. Come on, girls."

With that, Courtney went off with her group. Soon the other end of the gym was filled with the sound of her girls dribbling, passing, and making shots from the foul line.

Tipper's group was quiet. When would

they get a turn? No one asked for Tipper's autograph now. The girls just wanted to play basketball. They weren't going to improve if they were watching from the sidelines.

"Sorry, guys. I really goofed," Tipper told the girls. "But that doesn't mean we just have to sit here. Let's do some stretches. Then I can show you some things my college coach taught me about the ready position and about guarding. You don't need a ball for those. Bet you've never played basketball without a ball before!"

Soon Tipper's girls were having fun even without the ball.

"First I'm going to show you the ready position. Okay, everybody, line up and do what I do."

Tipper stood with her feet apart, knees bent, arms out, and hands curved as if she were holding a ball. She made the girls practice their ready positions quicker and quicker. "Relax. Hold. Ready position! Now I want you to run, then get into position when I say stop."

In no time the girls were able to get themselves into the ready position without even thinking about it.

"Okay, the next drill is guarding," Tipper said. "This is important, girls. You need to be as close as possible to the other player, but you can't touch her. I don't want my Fast Breakers giving up foul shots to the other team. Okay, let's try 'ghosting.' Pair up with another player. Pretend one of you is running to the backboard with the ball. The other girl shadows the runner like a ghost. Remember, no touching!"

The girls enjoyed this drill. Tipper made them shadow each other closer and closer, faster and faster. When anyone touched, she blew the whistle, and the "ghost" was out. After a while, Tipper hardly blew her whistle at all.

"Gee, I guess you really can have fun playing basketball without a basketball," Violet said when the girls took a break.

Tipper bit her lip. She looked over at Courtney's girls. They showed no sign of giving up the ball. "Well, there's only half an hour left. It's even more fun to play with a ball! I'll ask Courtney for it."

At eight-thirty, Courtney's group finally quit.

"Everybody drink plenty of water," Courtney told her group when they stopped playing. She threw the ball across the gym to Tipper. "It's all yours."

Tipper jumped to her feet. "Okay, girls. Now you can try out everything we've been practicing, only this time with a ball. Ready?"

"Ready!" Tipper's girls screamed.

Soon they, too, were passing, dribbling, and making baskets.

A short half hour later, Courtney blew her whistle again. "Time to go home."

"Do we have to leave?" Violet asked when Courtney came over. "Our group didn't get much of a chance to practice with the ball."

Courtney pointed to the clock. "Sorry, the manager told me we had to get everybody out by nine o'clock sharp." She looked at Tipper. "Maybe next time somebody will bring the storage room key so the whole team can play basketball."

Tipper said nothing. Her girls were silent as they filed out of the gym.

"Patsy, could you get my ball and stick it back in my gym bag?" Courtney asked. "I'll be ready in a minute."

Patsy picked up the basketball. "Would you unzip Courtney's bag, and I'll stuff it in?" she asked Jessie.

When Jessie held the bag open, she noticed something. "Look at this." She held up a key chain attached to the zipper pull. "One of the keys says, '*Storage Room*.' Courtney had her own key the whole time."

Violet ran over to the coach. "Courtney! Courtney! We just found the storage room key. It was on your gym bag."

Courtney didn't say anything right away.

"Is it the key for the storage room of this gym?" Tipper asked Courtney.

"There are a lot of keys on the chain.

One is for the storage room of my apartment building." With that, Courtney took her bag from Patsy. "Next time, Tipper, please bring your own key. The girls need to practice."

CHAPTER 4

A Big Letdown

At nine o'clock the next morning, the Alden children and the Nettleton twins were sound asleep.

However, Watch was not sound asleep, not at all. He was wide-awake and scratching at Jessie's bedroom door. He had heard Grandfather Alden out in the hallway. He wanted to be up and about, too.

Mr. Alden heard the whimpering and scratching. He slowly opened Jessie's door. Watch scooted out and ran downstairs.

"I'm going out shopping today," Mrs.

McGregor told Mr. Alden when he followed Watch into the kitchen.

Mr. Alden took Watch's leash from the hook on the back door. "Have a good time, Mrs. McGregor. I'm glad all the young people are sleeping late for a change. This basketball fever is wearing them out. As for the twins — they've been on the go since they arrived. Henry said they don't have any practices or appointments until this afternoon."

Mrs. McGregor put on her hat. "Last night, Buzz and Tipper told me not to make breakfast," she told Mr. Alden. "They said they were going to sleep late, then surprise the children with breakfast at the diner."

Mr. Alden smiled. "That's just the kind of surprise my grandchildren like."

Nearly all of Greenfield seemed to be enjoying breakfast at the Starlight Diner when the Aldens and the Nettleton twins arrived.

"Hello, Aldens!" the waitress said. "I recognize you two," she told the twins. "I saw your picture in the paper last night. Welcome back to Greenfield."

"Thanks," Buzz said. "It's good to be back. Especially here. Our whole team used to come to the Starlight Diner for your famous burgers after basketball games. I hope you have room today. It's pretty crowded in here."

The waitress picked up an armful of menus. She waved everyone over to the back. "You just got lucky. A group of construction workers just left. The big booth in the corner is free."

Benny looked up at Buzz. "It's not really free," he whispered. "You still have to pay."

Buzz laughed. "Good one, Benny. Well, I'm glad we don't have practice until later, you guys. It felt good to get a couple extra winks of sleep for a change."

Soo Lee thought about this. "I don't wink when I sleep. I shut my eyes all night."

Tipper squeezed the little girl's hand. "I don't wink when I sleep, either, Soo Lee."

Everyone slid into the big booth and picked up a menu.

Benny didn't have to read it. "I already know what I want," he announced.

"Let me guess," Buzz said. "Liver and onions, right?"

"No way!" Benny cried. "Waffles with big holes to pour the syrup in. That's what I'm having."

That's what *everyone* in the booth was having. The Starlight Diner was famous for its waffles.

"Well, dig in!" Buzz said when the waitress set the plates down a few minutes later.

The booth was quiet while everyone ate their delicious waffles. But no one could finish them. In a short time, the children put down their forks.

"Our eyes are bigger than our stomachs," Tipper said.

"I was hungry. But even I can't finish these giant waffles," Buzz said. "We won't be able to play basketball if we're too full. Right, Henry?"

"Right!" Henry answered. "We'll be doing a lot of running and jumping. It's better not to eat too much. The other players can't wait to meet you. They keep saying how lucky I am to have my own private coach."

Buzz set down his glass of orange juice. "I wish that were true. Tipper and I haven't helped any of you Aldens much for the last few days. I'm not so sure I like being famous anymore. All these appointments and appearances sure get in the way of basketball."

"I know," Tipper agreed. "I'm getting forgetful, we're so busy running around. I forgot the key to the gym storage room yesterday. I'd rather play basketball than be on television."

"You would?" Benny said. "I thought you liked being on television."

"Not as much as I like coaching the team," Tipper told the Aldens.

"Same here," Buzz said. "That's really why I came back to Greenfield, not to have my picture taken all the time." Buzz checked his watch. "We'd better get on the move. How about dropping off Henry and me at the sports center? It's almost time for my first practice with the Blazers. I don't want to keep them waiting."

When Tipper drove up to the sports center, Henry noticed how empty the place looked. "No one seems to be around. I'll run in and check if anyone from the team is here yet."

By the time Buzz unloaded the car, Henry was back. "The doors are locked. Do you have a key?"

"Oh, no, not missing keys again!" Tipper said with a groan.

Buzz jingled something in his pocket. "Right here. Frank Fowler gave me a set yesterday. Let's check around. It's not noon yet. We're a little early. Why don't you kids get out and shoot a few baskets until the rest of the Blazers get here."

The Aldens followed Buzz and Tipper.

Buzz put his key in the lobby door. "Ta-da! See, I brought my keys, not like some people I'm related to."

Tipper didn't like hearing this. "Don't

tease me about that, Buzz. I feel awful that I let down the girls."

Violet slipped her hand into Tipper's. "You didn't let us down. We had fun. I learned a lot — how to guard people and how to always be in the ready position. We didn't need a basketball. We just needed you."

Inside the sports center, a few workmen were painting on finishing touches.

"Hey, there, guys," Tom Hooper said when he saw the twins walk in with the Aldens.

Buzz gave Tom a big grin. "Good to see you again, Tom. I'm here to coach the Blazers this afternoon so we can beat those fearsome Rockets of yours."

Tom pointed to the hall clock with his paintbrush. "You sure you have afternoon practice, Buzz? The Blazers were all here around ten o'clock this morning looking for you. I couldn't let them into the gym. So they all kind of straggled off."

"What do you mean, Tom?" Buzz reached into his back pocket. He pulled out a piece of paper and unfolded it. "Here's the schedule Frank gave me a couple of days ago," he told Tom. "Doesn't that say noon?"

"Sorry, I'm not too good at figuring out schedules and such," Tom said. "I just show up when somebody tells me to."

Tipper looked over Buzz's shoulder. "It does say noon," she agreed when she read the schedule. "I wonder why the team came early. Maybe you can call up some of the boys and ask them to come back, Buzz."

"Sorry, that won't work out," Tom said. "After you didn't show up, the other paint-ers decided to do some touch-up work in the gym. The paint won't be dry for a few more hours. And tonight's no good, either. That's when I'm supposed to coach the Rockets in the gym. At least, I think that's what's on my schedule, if I can ever find it!"

Buzz looked upset. He checked the clock, then his schedule again. "I can't figure out what happened here. I planned all my ap-pointments around this piece of paper."

"Try the outdoor court in back," Tom

said. "Some of the boys had a basketball with them. A few of them decided to wait for you out there. That was awhile ago, though. I don't know if they're still there."

When the Aldens and twins got outside, Henry mentioned something he had been thinking about. "Tom doesn't ever seem to know what's going on. Wouldn't he have a copy of the same schedule as yours?"

"I noticed the same thing," Buzz answered. "Courtney and Frank seem to organize everything. Maybe Tom's too busy getting the sports center ready to keep his mind on the plans."

As Henry neared the outdoor court, he recognized a few boys sitting on a bench nearby. One boy sat there bouncing a basketball slowly, over and over. The two other boys looked up when Buzz, Tipper, and the Aldens arrived. The boys just sat there and didn't say a word.

"Hi!" Buzz said. "I'm Buzz Nettleton, one of your coaches. I think there was some mix-up about our practice."

The boy with the basketball stopped

bouncing. "Yeah, there was a mix-up, all right. We have a schedule saying to meet for practice at ten o'clock. My dad dropped me off here early and everything. I even brought my new basketball for you to sign."

"Sure thing," Buzz said. He reached into his pocket for a pen.

The boy looked at Buzz. He began bouncing the ball again. "Never mind."

Buzz didn't know what to say. "Listen, guys, I have to apologize. I guess the schedules were changed and nobody told you. But that doesn't mean we can't practice out here right now. How about it?"

A car horn blew before the boys could answer.

"Our ride is here," one of the boys said. "Besides, we already practiced. We got a whole lot of practice just sitting around waiting for you to show up."

"I don't blame the guys," Buzz said after the car drove away. "Somebody gave us the wrong schedules. I don't know if it was theirs or mine, but I plan to find out."

CHAPTER 5

Jessie's Good Idea

That night Buzz and Tipper finally sat down to one of Mrs. McGregor's home-cooked meals. At last, no interviews. No banquets. No meetings or plans. Just a quiet evening with the Aldens.

A very quiet evening.

Mr. Alden did his best to cheer up the twins. "Mistakes happen," he said when he noticed that they hadn't said much during dinner. "You two have been on the go from the minute you arrived. It's understandable that schedules and keys and such got mixed up. There's still plenty of time to coach the Blazers and Fast Breakers before their games."

Buzz pushed his cake around his plate without taking a bite. "We don't have that many practices scheduled, Mr. Alden. And we got off to a poor start. Tipper and I shouldn't have been running around so much. Then all these mix-ups wouldn't have happened."

"Did you call Frank Fowler?" Mr. Alden asked. "After all, he's the one who made up the schedules, right?"

"I called him when I got back this afternoon," Buzz said. "He said he told me about the schedule change a couple of days ago. There was so much going on that day. Tipper and I had our pictures taken for the newspaper with some of our old high school teammates. There were so many people around, I guess I just didn't focus on what Frank said."

"Same with Courtney and the storage room key," Tipper added. "That day was a blur for me, too."

Buzz put down his napkin. "I've got to figure out some way to make things up to the Blazers — extra practices or something."

"Same here," Tipper agreed. "Coaching isn't just teaching basketball skills. It's pulling the team together. That's what I learned from my high school and college coaches. I want to be just like them."

All this time, the Alden children sat and listened. Just because of a few mix-ups, their new friends weren't having a very good time.

"I have an idea," Jessie said. "Do you both have a whole day free in the next couple of days?"

"Saturday we're free," Buzz said. "For some reason, we're not scheduled to be famous celebrities that day. No picture-taking. No television."

Jessie's face brightened. "Good. What about organizing the first-ever Nettleton Basketball Clinic for Saturday? We could hold it right here in Grandfather's backyard. You could schedule different drills for dif-

ferent times. I know we don't have a whole
court, but you could teach lots of skills like
you did with us when you first got here."

Buzz gave this some thought. "A clinic,
hmmm?"

"Like a doctor clinic?" Soo Lee asked. "I
don't want to get a shot."

This made everyone smile.

Tipper put her arm around the little girl.
"You wouldn't get a shot, Soo Lee. But you
would make a lot of basketball shots, just
like you did the other day. A basketball
clinic helps players practice skills one at a
time. No doctors, no shots. Just fun."

Suddenly Buzz's face brightened. "You
know, I brought some training tapes from
my college. We could show those as part of
the clinic."

"We can run an extension cord from the
garage to the boxcar and hook up Grandfather's portable television and playback machine out there," Henry suggested.

The twins were all caught up in the
Aldens' plans now.

"We'll mix up the teams," Buzz said.

"The Blazers and Fast Breakers can do the drills together with kids from other teams. A clinic just might help us make up the practice time our team missed. Good idea, Aldens!"

Tipper wondered about something. "Should we check with Courtney and Frank and Tom? I mean, a clinic isn't really part of the plans they have scheduled."

Buzz shook his head. "The clinic doesn't have to be part of the plans. Let's just call kids up and tell them about it. Anybody can come."

By this time Buzz and Tipper had spread out some paper and pencils to write down their plans.

"If we run the drills in sets, kids can start whenever they arrive," Tipper said. "We could probably fit in three sets of drills. That way it won't get too crowded in the backyard." Tipper put down her pencil. "Whoa, stop! We haven't even asked Mr. Alden if it's okay to fill his yard with all these basketball players."

Mr. Alden put down his coffee cup. "I

like seeing my yard filled with youngsters. Why, what's the good of having a big yard if people don't use it?"

Mr. Alden got his wish. By noon on Saturday, basketball players from all over Greenfield were in the backyard doing drills. In one part of the driveway, Buzz showed players how to dribble the ball while running. Tipper showed some older children how to make shots from the foul line. In the boxcar, Henry had set up Mr. Alden's portable television and a playback machine. About half a dozen players were inside the boxcar watching training tapes from Buzz's college. The clinic was a huge success.

"This is so much fun, I'm staying all day," Patsy Cutter told Jessie. "I want to be the champ of the Fast Breakers."

When Patsy went off to practice her foul shots, Jessie turned to Violet. "I was hoping Patsy would only stay for one set of drills. That's what I told everyone. More kids showed up at the clinic than we expected. Some players haven't had even one chance for Tipper to coach them."

Henry joined the girls outside. "Whew, I can't believe how many people are here. Buzz asked me to call up Courtney, Frank, and Tom. We definitely need more coaches!"

Right after Henry phoned the other coaches, a cameraman and reporter arrived from the local television station. The Nettleton Basketball Clinic was big news in Greenfield!

The reporter looked a little rushed and out of breath. "At last! I finally caught up with you two," she said to the twins. "My cameraman and I waited for you for about an hour at the sports center. When you didn't show up, we started calling around. We tracked you down here."

Tipper and Buzz looked confused.

"Why did you think we'd be at the sports center?" Buzz wanted to know.

"Didn't you get my message?" the woman asked. "I told someone at the center that we would meet you there at ten o'clock today and to call me if you couldn't make it."

Buzz shook his head. "We didn't hear a thing about this. We're in the middle of running a clinic. We really can't do an interview right now."

"Why not?" the reporter asked. "Your basketball clinic makes an even better story. After all, you did come to Greenfield to help out with the sports center. This clinic will give it even more attention."

"I guess we don't have a choice," Buzz told Tipper.

"Okay. First we want to film Tipper with her Most Valuable Player trophy," the reporter said. "Is it around?"

Tipper didn't move. "Can't you just show the two of us helping the kids? After all, isn't that the whole point of your coming here?"

"Sure," the reporter said. "But you're the first Greenfield player to get the MVP award. That is big news!"

"I'll go get it," Patsy Cutter offered when she overheard the reporter.

"You know where it is?" Tipper asked, surprised to hear this.

"Well, I saw it when Jessie and I were in her room," Patsy answered. "When I borrowed a pair of shorts from her."

"Good. Bring it down here," the reporter told Patsy.

When Patsy returned, the cameraman was taping Buzz showing several players how to dribble.

Patsy handed the trophy to Tipper. "Here it is."

Seeing this, the cameraman stopped filming Buzz and aimed his camera at Tipper instead.

"There," the cameraman told Tipper. "Just hold it like that while I get more tape rolling."

Buzz tried to get his players back to playing basketball. No luck. They all wanted to be on television. While the cameraman taped, several children stood near Tipper and waved or made funny faces at the camera. They were going to be on television, too!

"Buzz looks upset," Violet whispered to

Jessie when they came over to see what was going on. "It's just like the day when we kept asking about Tipper's award."

Buzz wasn't the only person upset about Tipper's award. By this time, Courtney Post and Frank Fowler had arrived to help with the clinic. But there was no coaching, no practicing, and no drills going when Courtney and Frank showed up. Instead everyone was watching the television crew filming Tipper and her award. Finally the cameraman waved Buzz into the picture, too.

The reporter faced the camera. "And it looks as if the Nettleton twins are headed for victory again — not as Most Valuable Players, but as Most Valuable Coaches in Greenfield."

"Oh, no," Henry whispered to Jessie. "Frank and Courtney won't like that." Henry went over to them before any more damage was done. "Thanks for showing up on such short notice. We really need your help. We didn't expect so many kids to come."

Jessie tried to explain what happened. "The television people heard about the clinic when they went to the sports center. Then they came here. Buzz and Tipper didn't invite them. All they wanted to do was make up for the practices they missed. When so many kids showed up, they thought you might want to help out."

"Great timing," Courtney said. "We show up just in time to be in the audience for two coaches who don't even live in Greenfield anymore. I've got better ways to spend my Saturdays."

"Me, too," Frank said.

At last the television people left. The children flocked around Tipper to get a close look at her famous trophy.

"It's real silver," one girl from the Clipper team said.

"Of course it's real silver," Patsy Cutter told the girl.

"You should keep it in a safe place like a bank or something, with guards," another girl said, touching the tall, heavy trophy.

Buzz blew his whistle. "The interview is

over. Everybody who wants to do some drills, line up near the backboard."

"Right," Tipper said, sticking the trophy inside the boxcar. "Let's play basketball. That's what we're all here for."

"Anybody who wants to learn how to do championship layups should go with Coach Fowler," Buzz said. "He's the best layup player Greenfield ever had."

"Except for Courtney Post," Tipper said to the players who were trying to decide what to do next. "Her layups are amazing. Maybe Frank and Courtney can take over all the layup drills."

When they heard this, Frank Fowler and Courtney Post finally stopped looking so upset. Buzz and Tipper were famous for being famous. But Courtney and Frank were famous for their layups.

Buzz and Tipper moved out of the way of the two coaches. For the next hour they stayed in the boxcar, showing some of the kids training tapes. They wanted to give Frank and Courtney a chance to be the star coaches now.

*   *   *

By three o'clock, everyone was worn-out.

"What a day!" Henry said. "We had more people than at the sports center — almost, anyway."

"Thanks for coming," Tipper told Frank and Courtney. "We couldn't have done it without you. Especially after those television people showed up. That was the last thing we needed. From now until the sports center opens, all I want to do is coach basketball."

"Me, too," Buzz said.

"Mind if we take a look at the training tapes before we leave?" Courtney asked Buzz. "Frank and I want to see how your coach teaches defense positions."

"Sure, the tapes are on a shelf in the boxcar," Buzz said. "Just pop them into the machine."

"See you Monday," Frank told everyone. "We'll turn off the television after we're done."

"So things worked out after all," Henry said after the Aldens went inside the house. "The clinic was a good idea, Jessie."

"Not a good idea — a great idea," Buzz said. "Except for all those TV people showing up, we taught everybody a whole lot of basketball."

The clinic had been a hit. The Aldens and the Nettleton twins decided to sit down and plan another one. They were so busy talking about what they would do next time, nobody paid any mind to Watch. He was barking and barking at the kitchen window.

"It's only Patsy out there, still practicing," Jessie said. "She's probably hoping you'll come out and coach her some more, Tipper."

Tipper yawned. "I'm all coached out. All I can think of is a hot shower and a nap. I'm afraid Patsy's on her own."

CHAPTER 6

Double Trouble

All the Aldens loved having the Nettleton twins as houseguests. But for Jessie, their visit was extra special. She was sharing her room with Tipper. Each night, after they turned out the lights, the two of them would talk in the dark until they drifted off to sleep. Jessie loved these cozy times.

"I feel so much better after running the clinic today," Tipper said. "I finally got to be the kind of coach my coaches have been to me. They taught me so much. Now it's my turn to teach kids what I know about basketball."

"I learned a lot from you and Courtney today," Jessie said. She stretched and yawned before curling up under the covers. "I'm tired, but it's a good kind of tired. That chair drill you did with us was fun. Sitting in a chair and trying to make baskets taught me how to stretch my arm way out and follow through."

"Follow through," Tipper said. "That's the key to everything — passing, shooting, dribbling."

Jessie's voice slowed down. "The key. I'm glad Mr. Fowler gave you that extra key for the gym today. Do you think Courtney ever gave you one in the first place?"

Tipper thought about this. "I honestly can't remember. I'm not going to bring it up with her again. All I want is for the two of us to work together. If only she would forget that we used to play on opposing teams."

"Courtney did seem a little jealous, seeing you with your trophy and all," Jessie said.

Tipper was practically asleep now. "That trophy. I can't wait until it's in a glass case at the sports center."

The room was almost silent now, except for Watch's gentle snoring.

Then Tipper sat up in bed. "Omigosh!" she said all of a sudden. "The trophy! I forgot all about it. Now, where did I put it after the TV people left?"

Jessie turned on the bedside lamp. The girls blinked at the sudden light. Tipper and Jessie stared at the bookcase.

"I forgot to put it back," Tipper said, fully awake now. She checked under both beds, then in the closet. "Let me think. After the interview all the kids were fussing over it. I thought it might bother Courtney and Buzz."

"I know!" Jessie cried. "You put it in the boxcar right before Courtney and Mr. Fowler started the layup drills. Remember?"

Tipper remembered. In no time, she put

on her slippers. "I'm going out to the box-car to get it now. Otherwise I'll be up all night thinking about it."

Jessie stepped into her slippers, too. She grabbed the flashlight she kept by her bed. Watch followed the girls down through the dark house.

The moon was shining. The backyard was all silvery. The girls tiptoed out to the boxcar.

Jessie slid open the door. She waved her flashlight this way and that. "I don't see it. Maybe somebody put it away for safe-keeping," Jessie told Tipper to make her friend feel better. "I bet that's what happened."

"I hope you're right," Tipper said.

The girls returned to the house and went back to bed.

But Tipper didn't drift off to sleep easily. Her trophy seemed to have a curse on it. The curse wouldn't go away until she gave the trophy away. And she couldn't do that until she found it.

*   *   *

The next morning Tipper and Jessie stumbled into the kitchen for breakfast. They were pale, and they were both tired.

"My goodness, you girls look as if you haven't slept a wink," Mrs. McGregor said.

Mr. Alden looked up from his morning paper. "Maybe you should go back to bed and sleep in a little longer," he suggested. "Is anything the matter?"

"Tipper's trophy is missing," Jessie announced. "She put it in the boxcar yesterday. We went out there last night, but it wasn't there. It's not in my room, either. We're going to look around the house and outside now that it's daytime."

"Soo Lee and I will help," Benny said. "We're good at finding things. We have sharp eyes."

Tipper smiled for the first time that morning. "If anyone can find my trophy, I know you Aldens can."

But the Aldens had no luck, either. Benny and Soo Lee checked under every piece of furniture indoors and every tree and bush outdoors. The older children searched the garage and the back porch. The trophy was nowhere to be found.

"How did it wind up missing?" Henry wondered. "Everybody was around all afternoon yesterday. Unless . . . well, I mean, Frank and Courtney were the last ones in the boxcar. Remember? They were in there watching the training tapes."

Tipper twisted the corners of her napkin. She seemed about to say something, but the words wouldn't come out.

"Why don't we just call them up?" Jessie asked. "It can't hurt to ask."

Tipper was lost in thought. "It could hurt to ask, Jessie. If they didn't take it, they'll be upset that I suspect them. Buzz and I are just starting to get along with Courtney and Frank. Let's just wait until Buzz gets back. He had a meeting at the sports center this morning. I'll ask him if he's seen it."

Mr. Alden put down his newspaper. "I wish I'd known the trophy was missing. I drove Buzz to the center, but he didn't mention it. He should be back in a while. Tom Hooper is going to drop him off."

Tipper couldn't touch the food on her plate. "You know what? I'll just get restless waiting for him. I need to get out of the house. Jessie, why don't I drive you to that sporting goods store. I know you wanted to exchange those sneakers you bought for a bigger size."

"Good idea. Violet and I need some crew socks, too." Jessie ran upstairs to get her new sneakers. When she came back down, everyone was outside, standing by the twins' car.

"Here, put your shopping bag in the trunk," Tipper said, lifting the lid. "When all of you Aldens are in the car, there's not much room for anything else!"

Tipper was about to slam down the trunk lid when Buzz came into the backyard. "Hey, you found my hiding place!" he said. "It's not easy hiding things from you Aldens."

Tipper and the children stood in front of the empty trunk.

"What are you talking about, Buzz?" Tipper asked.

"Your MVP trophy," Buzz answered. "Isn't that what you're looking for? I stuck it in there yesterday. Patsy was showing it off to other kids in the boxcar. I got worried it would get scratched or something. Whoa, what's that look you're giving me, Tip?"

Tipper swallowed hard. "But why did you put it in the car? When the doors are unlocked anybody can pull the lever from under the front seat and open the trunk."

"I planned to go back and get it. But . . . well, I forgot. Sorry about that," Buzz said. He looked at the Aldens. "Hey, were you guys spying on me? Is that how you figured out it was in there?"

No one answered for a long time.

Tipper stepped away from the car. She pointed to the empty trunk. "There's no trophy in there, Buzz."

Buzz's face went white. His smile disappeared from his face. "What do you mean, it's not there? You're kidding, right?"

The Aldens moved away from the car, too.

"Take a look, Buzz," Tipper said. "The trunk is empty."

Buzz didn't speak. He went around, opened the doors, and checked inside the car. Then he looked under the car and all around the garage.

"Don't bother. The Aldens and I already checked every inch of the garage, the boxcar, the whole yard, and the entire house," Tipper told her brother. "We've looked everywhere."

Buzz stared at his sister. "Please don't look at me like that, Tip. I was trying to keep your trophy safe. Honest. That's why I put it in the trunk. It wasn't the best place, but I was going to bring it up to your room first thing. Then I got so busy, I forgot."

Tipper couldn't seem to look Buzz in the eye. She stood there and just stared down at her sneakers. "I guess it's my fault. I should have put it away myself. And now it's gone."

In a minute, Buzz was gone, too. He

walked down the driveway and disappeared down the street.

The children followed Tipper inside.

"What happened to your shopping trip?" Mr. Alden asked when everyone came into the kitchen. "Is something wrong?"

"Buzz took Tipper's trophy yesterday," Benny said. "But now he doesn't know where it is."

"I see," Mr. Alden said quietly.

Tipper tried to explain to Mr. Alden what had happened. "Buzz told me he saw Patsy showing off the trophy during the clinic yesterday. So he put it in the trunk and forgot to tell me. I mean, it's the most important thing I own. How could he forget? It's almost as if he wants it to disappear. And now it has."

Mr. Alden spoke gently. "Do you think he's done this on purpose?"

Tipper swallowed hard. "If it was anything else but the trophy, I would say no. We've always known everything about each other. That's the way twins are . . . until now. Ever since I got the award, Buzz has been different, not like his old self."

"He sure does act touchy about that trophy," Henry said.

"It's impossible to talk to him about it," Tipper agreed. "I don't want to accuse him, but this is the second time he's left the trophy in the car when it's been unlocked."

"Come sit down and have some breakfast," Mr. Alden said. "I'm sure we can help you figure this out."

Soo Lee patted Tipper's hand. "Benny and I are good finders. We found Violet's bracelet on the driveway."

"Once we found an old violin that was missing," Benny said. "And lots of other stuff people were looking for."

"What if we put up some Lost and Found posters?" Violet asked Tipper. "I could draw a picture of the trophy. I remember what it looked like."

This helped Tipper feel better, but only a little. "That's a good idea. Of course, if Buzz . . . Well, never mind. Besides, Buzz and I can't let ourselves think about the trophy too much — not with your championship games coming up. I'll just have to deal with it after the games are over. I'm going upstairs to rest."

Tipper left the kitchen. The Aldens could barely hear her footsteps. The children were quiet. Winning a big silver trophy sure didn't seem like much fun anymore.

CHAPTER 7

One-on-One

Over the next few days, Tipper and Buzz avoided the whole sore subject of the missing trophy. It was time to coach the Fast Breakers and the Blazers for the championships. The twins filled everyone's days with practices, clinics, and drills. If they were upset with each other, they tried not to show it. Basketball came first.

But the Aldens thought a lot about Tipper's missing trophy. They put Violet's Lost and Found posters all over Greenfield. Maybe somebody knew something about where it might be. They just couldn't accept that Buzz had anything to do with its disappearance.

"You know, Patsy was up in my room acting kind of funny the day she borrowed my shorts," Jessie said one afternoon when the twins were out. "She got all upset when I asked her about it. I feel funny bringing the subject up again, but maybe she had something to do with the trophy. After the other kids left, she was still outside playing basketball. Remember?"

Violet had some thoughts, too. "Well, lots of other kids besides Patsy were holding and touching it."

"If you ask me, Courtney and Frank Fowler could have taken it if they saw Buzz put it in the car," Henry suggested. "Look how bothered they are that the twins get so much attention. Too bad Tipper doesn't want to ask them about the trophy. I guess she doesn't want more problems with them."

"You're right, Henry," Jessie said. "Well, let's just hope someone who knows something about the trophy will see our posters and give us a call."

But no one called about the missing trophy. And the Aldens had very little time to think about it until the championship games were over.

More than anything, Buzz and Tipper wanted to help the Fast Breakers and the Blazers to win their own trophies. Every night before dinner they coached the Aldens for a few minutes.

"I hope no one gets too upset that you give us extra help," Henry told Buzz one evening when they were playing one-on-one in the backyard.

"Only a little extra help," Buzz said. "Besides, it gives Tipper and me some extra practice, too. No doubt about it, you Aldens give us a good workout. Don't forget, we have to be in good shape for our fund-raising game on Opening Day."

Henry zoomed past Buzz. "And it's . . . in!" he cried when his quick layup circled the rim then dropped through the net.

"Good one, Henry!" Buzz said. "If you make shots like that against the Hot Shots tomorrow, the Blazers will win the championship."

Henry and Buzz went in to get a drink of water. It was the girls' turn to practice.

Jessie and Violet went outside to wait for Tipper. They were surprised to see Patsy Cutter in the backyard. She was practicing shots from the foul line.

"Hi, Patsy," Violet said. She gave her friend a big smile. "You're just in time to practice with Jessie and me. Tipper will be out in a second."

Patsy didn't look too happy to see Violet or Jessie. "Some of the Fast Breakers think it's not fair that you get Tipper to yourselves all the time. I decided to come for extra help."

"It's okay with us," Jessie said. "Why don't you work out with Tipper by yourself? You're such a good player, Violet and I can learn a lot just by watching the two of you play."

This seemed to make Patsy feel better.

Soon Tipper joined her for some one-on-one basketball.

"I'm getting a real workout here," Tipper told Patsy as she tried to get the ball away. "You're pretty good at faking me out."

Patsy made another basket.

Violet and Jessie were cheering. "Good shot, Patsy!" Violet said, proud of her friend.

Patsy made one more basket. It went in. She'd beaten Tipper Nettleton!

"Great playing, Patsy," Tipper said. "Courtney's taught you a lot. The Blue Stars girls had better watch out. Thanks for playing with me. I need the practice before I meet Courtney across the court during the fund-raising game next week."

Patsy put her basketball in her sports bag. "Thanks, Tipper." She turned to Jessie. "I brought back your shorts. Do you have the ones I left here?"

"They're still in the upstairs bathroom," Jessie told her. "On the towel bar."

Patsy picked up her sports bag. "I'll leave these on your bed and go get mine."

Jessie got up, too. "I'll come with you."

"That's okay," Patsy said. "I know where to go."

"I have to get something, anyway," Jessie told Patsy.

Patsy reached into her bag. "Well, never mind. Here are the shorts I borrowed. I'll get mine some other time."

Jessie took the shorts. "No problem. I'll bring them to our next practice."

The next day, the Blazers and the Hot Shots met on the courts of the Greenfield High School gym, where the championship games were being held. Henry and his team were down on the court. Tipper and the other Aldens were up in the bleachers, waiting for the second half of the game to start.

The two teams were a good match. At halftime the scoreboard said Blazers, 22, Hot Shots, 22.

Buzz stood in front of the Blazers for a pep talk.

A player named Jake Reed raised his hand. "I didn't foul number fifteen. Hon-

estly, Buzz. But Mr. Fowler blew the whistle on me, anyway."

"And when somebody fouled me, Mr. Fowler didn't catch it," Henry said. "What do we do if it happens again?"

Buzz thought hard. He'd been playing basketball a lot longer than the Blazers. He knew better than to question the referee. "Just play the best basketball you can," he told his team. "Don't get too close to anybody. That way you can't foul them, and they can't foul you. If you play good ball the way I taught you, you'll make all your points without any fouls."

Halftime was over. The Blazers and Hot Shots circled for the toss-up. The buzzer went off. Henry tipped the ball to Jake, who passed it to another Blazer. Frank Fowler blew his whistle. He signaled for the Blazers to hand the ball over to the Hot Shots.

"I can't believe it!" Jessie said when Frank Fowler made this call. "The Blazers' ball was inside the lines when they passed it, right, Tipper?"

Tipper rested her chin on her fists. "Whew! I don't believe what I'm seeing, either. Frank Fowler keeps making a lot of calls against the Blazers."

"Is there anything Buzz can do?" Violet asked Tipper.

Tipper kept her eyes on the court. "Not much. If he complains, it might upset Mr. Fowler. All Buzz can do is help his players stay calm and play the best basketball they can."

That's exactly how Buzz coached the Blazers from the sidelines. Though Frank Fowler missed seeing several fouls against the Blazers, Buzz didn't question the referee. He just cheered on his team.

With a minute left in the game, the score was tied at 46–46.

The game went into overtime. The two teams went basket for basket during overtime.

Then Henry got the rebound. With just another few seconds left on the clock, Henry made a basket.

"It's in!" the Aldens screamed from their

seats. "The Blazers are ahead by two points!"

Tipper chewed on her thumbnail. "All the Blazers have to do is keep the Hot Shots from scoring. This is where all those guarding drills Buzz did with the Blazers will pay off."

The gym was wild with noise and cheering. The Blazers and Hot Shots had never played a better game. The Hot Shots player with the ball looked for chances to pass or throw. But everywhere he looked, a Blazer guarded a Hot Shots player. Finally the Hot Shots player tried to shoot.

"Foul!" Frank Fowler called out, pointing to a Blazer guard.

The Blazers fans groaned. No one had seen the guard touch the player.

"He didn't touch him, did he, Tipper?" Violet asked.

Tipper shook her head. "I know he didn't. Everybody else knows he didn't, too. But that's what Frank called. Now the Hot Shots guy gets two foul shots."

The gym was completely silent now. The

Hot Shots player stood at the foul line. He made his first throw. The ball bounced off the rim.

"Whew," Jessie said. "The Blazers are still ahead." She crossed her fingers.

The player took another foul shot. This one circled the rim for the longest time. Was it going to go in?

"He missed!" Tipper cried when the ball dropped off the rim onto the court.

When the final buzzer went off, the crowd seemed to explode.

"The Blazers won! The Blazers won!" the Aldens and other Blazers fans yelled and screamed.

The Aldens scrambled down the bleachers to the court. They hugged Henry. They hugged Buzz.

"You're the champions!" Tipper said, hugging Buzz over and over. "You guys did it."

Friends and family and sports photographers took pictures and talked to the team. Then the mayor came out and presented the boys' league trophy to Buzz. He passed it down the line to his players. Finally, when all the picture-taking was over, the Blazers left the gym.

Tipper and the Aldens waited outside the locker room. Henry and Buzz came out in their street clothes a few minutes later.

Buzz gave Henry a friendly punch in the shoulder. "Great game, Henry. You guys did everything I taught you."

"I did everything but guard people without having fouls called against me," Henry said. "I can't believe how many fouls Mr. Fowler called. I don't think the Blazers committed half of them, either."

Buzz slowed down. "Listen, that happens to the best of teams. You can't predict what a ref is going to do. Sometimes the calls go your way. Sometimes they go the other way. I have to say, though, that I've never seen so many fouls called that I disagreed with."

Everyone passed the lockers where the referees and coaches kept their things.

"Speaking of disagreeable, look at Mr. Fowler," Henry whispered.

Frank Fowler stood in front of a locker.

He was dumping his things into his bag. In went his whistle. In went his referee shoes. In went his striped hat. He finally picked up his bag and muttered to himself all the way out the door.

"Anybody looking at Frank Fowler would think he lost the game instead of refereed it. That's pretty strange," said Buzz.

"Well, Buzz," Henry said, "the Blazers won the game fair and square thanks to your coaching. There's nothing strange about that!"

CHAPTER 8

Sneaky Sneakers

When Jessie and Violet walked into the sports center the next day, Tom Hooper was up on his ladder painting the ceiling.

"Hi, Tom," Tipper called out. "Looks as if you're almost done. How are you?"

Tom didn't answer, so Tipper and the Aldens kept walking down the hall.

"Hey, wait!" Tom called after them. "I just remembered something. Frank gave me a note for you, Tipper."

Everyone turned around. Tom came

down from his ladder. He searched the pocket of his painter's pants. "Now, what did I do with it?"

"Do with what?" Jessie asked.

"Frank's piece of paper . . . mmm . . . let me see." Tom emptied his pockets but found nothing. Finally he picked up a piece of paper from the floor. "Whew. It fell out of my pocket. Frank says this is very important. Sorry, I almost forgot." He handed Tipper a paint-splattered, wrinkled note.

Tipper read it aloud.

Dear Tipper,
The Blue Stars' coach just came down with the flu. Since the Fast Breakers team has two coaches, you and Courtney, I have assigned Courtney to coach the Blue Stars until the championship game.

Frank Fowler

"Looks as if it's just us Fast Breakers chickens," Tipper told the girls.

Violet and Jessie looked at each other. They didn't mind this new change of plans

at all. They knew one thing: Practice with Tipper alone would be a lot more fun from now on.

All their other teammates, except one, cheered when Tipper announced that she was now the Fast Breakers' only coach. Only Patsy Cutter seemed to mind. She loved Tipper, but she also loved having two coaches to give her lots of attention.

All through practice Patsy followed Tipper around and begged for extra help. But that wasn't Tipper's way of doing things.

"Sorry, Patsy," Tipper repeated. "I know you want me to work with you on the power drill again, but that's a one-player drill. Today we're only doing team drills. Now that Courtney's with the Blue Stars, I have to work more with our whole team."

"But . . . but . . ." Patsy protested. "If the really good players don't get special drills, we might not be the best like you."

Tipper put her arm around Patsy's shoulders. "Being the best player means helping the team to be the best."

Patsy sighed. She couldn't help it. She

wanted Tipper Nettleton to herself. But Patsy didn't have any choice. She lined up behind the other Fast Breakers. It was time for a team drill.

The Fast Breakers practiced for an hour. Then the lights flickered on and off. The girls stopped playing.

"Time for the Blue Stars' practice," Courtney yelled across the gym. Her hand was still on the light switch. "It's two o'clock."

Patsy, Violet, Jessie, and some of the other girls went over to say hello to their old coach.

"I wish we still had two coaches," Patsy complained to Courtney. "I need special help. We only have one coach now. I can't work on my power drill or the wall drill."

"That's the way it goes," Courtney said, none too friendly to the Fast Breakers now. "Tell your teammates to move along. The Blue Stars have to practice now."

Right up to the playoffs, Courtney treated the Fast Breakers like strangers. If their practice ran over just a few seconds, she complained.

"Don't mind Courtney," Tipper told the Fast Breakers. "Some coaches are tough like that. They want everyone to be afraid of their team. That's the way Courtney's old Warwick High School team played. We were terrified of them. In the end, they won some games, and we won some others. It's two different ways of coaching."

"We like your way," Violet said.

Patsy Cutter wasn't so sure. "I like your way, too, Tipper. But don't you think it's a good idea to build up some players the other team is afraid of?" she asked. "You know — make some of us so awesome, the other team gets nervous?"

Tipper laughed. "Do you have anybody in mind?"

Patsy finally laughed, too. "Well, if you change your mind, I can be pretty scary."

Tipper Nettleton laughed. "I don't want scary players, just good ones like you who work as a team."

*   *   *

When the day of the championship game arrived, the Aldens were excited, but also a little nervous.

At breakfast that morning, Violet pushed her scrambled eggs around her plate, unable to eat them. "I can't believe we're going to play in front of all those people," she said. "I'm so nervous. I almost wish Patsy and Jessie and the other best players would play the whole game."

"Hush!" Tipper said. "Put that thought from your mind, Violet. I know what will make you feel better. Let's do a quick work-out in back. When you see how well you practice, your confidence will bounce right back. Come on now."

Out in back, Violet tried out everything Tipper had taught her. Tipper helped her guard and pass and dribble and shoot until she was playing smoothly.

"You're right," Violet told Tipper when they finally stopped. "Now I know I can play against anyone, even the Blue Stars."

"Especially the Blue Stars," Tipper said before she and Violet went inside.

Jessie looked at the clock. "Only an hour and a half. What will we do until then?"

"Let's head over to the sports center to pick up our uniforms and basketball sneakers," Tipper suggested. "We have to take our things over to the Greenfield High gym before our game there."

"Good idea," Jessie said. "I'm too fidgety to stay home."

On the way over, Tipper helped the girls relax with some quiet music. "It's important to work yourselves hard, but it's also good to get your mind calm before a big game. That's what I always do."

But that wasn't what Courtney Post did with the Blue Stars. When Tipper and the Aldens walked into the sports center, Courtney was supervising some last-minute practice with two of her players. "Harder! Dribble it harder!" she yelled. "You don't want everybody to think you're the Blue Marshmallows, do you? Don't be afraid to look a little mean. It throws everybody off guard."

"They look scary," Violet whispered, starting to lose a little of her confidence.

"No, not scary, *miserable*," Jessie said.

Courtney noticed Tipper and the Aldens standing there.

"The office is unlocked," Courtney shouted at Tipper. "I sent my team's things over to the Greenfield High School gym with Frank. He's going to be the referee. We're leaving for the high school in a minute. Make sure you get your players there on time, too. You don't want to forfeit the game!"

"Ugh!" Tipper said with a groan after Courtney left. "Now, why did Courtney have to go and say that? I'm totally confident about everybody's playing. What I don't like much is getting everything ready — the equipment, the paperwork, the scoring sheets. I wish the sports center was ready so we could play the game here."

Violet patted Tipper's arm. "Don't worry. Jessie can help. She's always super-organized. She even lines up her slippers in one direction next to her bed every night."

Jessie laughed. "I thought everyone did that!"

The girls followed Tipper into the office. The room was still a little messy, with construction equipment cluttering up the small area.

"Can you get both duffel bags from the closet?" Tipper asked Jessie and Violet. "The uniforms and sneakers are in the bags. Oh, and grab a couple basketballs, just in case. You never know. I'll get the stopwatch and the papers we need for the game."

Jessie opened the closet door. "Did you mean this closet, Tipper?" she said. "There are only a couple of ladders and a bunch of paint cans in here."

Tipper came over. "Oh, no! The duffel bags were right here when we finished practice last night. I even put a name tag on each of them so no one would take them by mistake. I didn't want the team bags to get mixed up with anybody else's things."

"We'll go find Tom or Courtney," Jessie told Tipper.

"Tom? Tom?" Jessie called out. But the

only answer she heard was the sound of her own voice echoing back.

Violet ran to the lobby. She looked out the front doors. "Oh, no, Courtney just left."

Tipper and the Aldens were alone in the empty building.

"What should we do?" Jessie asked.

Tipper checked her watch. "Let's split up and check every unlocked room and closet in this building. Maybe the painters moved our bags somewhere else."

The girls split up. They raced through the dark halls. Most of the rooms and closets were locked.

When Violet and Jessie met Tipper in the lobby again, they were all empty-handed.

"All I can guess is that Tom or Frank took our duffel bags to the high school gym earlier," Tipper said, checking her watch again. "Let's keep our fingers crossed. We'd better get a move on. The game starts in about forty-five minutes."

CHAPTER 9

Go Team!

As she drove along, Tipper kept to the speed limit, but Jessie could see she was gripping the wheel. "I should have searched the office for a note or something," Tipper told the girls. "If Tom or Frank took our bags, they probably left a note."

"Maybe Mr. Fowler would, but Tom is so forgetful, I don't think he would remember to do that," Jessie pointed out.

When Tipper and the Aldens arrived at the Greenfield High School gym, they were disappointed. Frank had only delivered the Blue Stars' bags. The Fast Breakers' bags were nowhere to be seen, and the game was starting very soon.

"Finally!" Patsy Cutter said with relief when she saw Tipper and the Aldens. "The whole team was wondering where you guys were. They're in the locker room waiting for their uniforms and basketball sneakers. The Blue Stars are already out on the court warming up. What happened, anyway?"

"I'll tell you in a minute," Tipper said. "Ask the girls to meet me in the hallway outside the gym, okay? I need to speak to everyone without the Blue Stars around."

"There's not enough time," Patsy said. "We have to change."

Tipper took a deep breath. "I just need five minutes, Patsy. Please bring the team out to the hallway."

When Patsy passed back through the gym with the girls, Courtney and the Blue Stars were already warming up. They stared at the Fast Breakers. Why were they still in their street clothes? Weren't they going to warm up before the big game?

Tipper stood in front of her team in the hallway. "There's been a mix-up with the uniforms and sneakers," she began. "We're just waiting for Tom to show up. I'm counting on him to get here any minute."

"Are we going to forfeit the game?" Patsy asked. "We can't play without our uniforms or basketball sneakers. What's going on?"

Tipper shook her head. "I don't know. Sometimes I feel as if someone is making these mix-ups happen."

At that moment, Courtney came out. "It's less than half an hour to game time."

"We know, we know," Patsy said miserably to her old coach.

"Never mind us, Courtney," Tipper said. "We'll be there." Tipper Nettleton wasn't about to let this upset her girls. "Now listen. Remember the drills we did? I want you to take a couple of basketballs, then go to the outside court and warm up. Patsy and Jessie will coach you. The second the bags get here, zoom into the locker room, change, and get ready to play. We're going to win, right?"

There was a long pause.

"Right!" Jessie and Violet shouted.

"Right!" the others finally joined in as they followed Patsy and the Aldens outside.

Inside the gym, the bleachers were packed. Buzz and the Aldens noticed that only the Blue Stars were out on the court.

"Where are the Fast Breakers?" Henry asked Buzz.

"I'm going to find out," Buzz said. "Something's wrong. Tipper knows how important the warm-up is. Her players will be tense for the game if they don't practice first."

"I'll come with you," Henry said.

They found Tipper by a pay phone in the hallway. She was waiting nervously for a woman to finish a call. "Buzz, Henry — thank goodness you're both here. We may have to forfeit the game. The duffel bags with our uniforms and sneakers haven't ar-rived. Did either one of you see them the last time you were at the sports center?"

Henry's mouth dropped. "The team doesn't have its uniforms?"

"Oh, no! That's an automatic forfeit," Buzz said. "Do you want me to go back to the sports center to look for the bags?"

Tipper shook her head. "It's too late for that. I'm trying to reach Tom Hooper. He put some of the paint equipment in the closet at the sports center where I'd stored the duffel bags. I'm hoping he's on his way here with the bags."

At last the person using the pay phone hung up. Tipper dropped some coins in. She quickly punched in Tom Hooper's home number. She shifted from foot to foot.

Tipper put down the receiver. "Tom's not there. How can I break this to the team? They've practiced so hard. Hey, why are you smiling, Buzz?"

Buzz looked over Tipper's shoulder and kept on smiling. "Look who's running down the hall! And check out what he's got in his hands."

Tipper whirled around. Tom Hooper was

stumbling down the hall as best he could with a heavy duffel bag in each hand.

Tipper broke into a run. She grabbed the bags from Tom. "Thank goodness you're here! We were looking all over for you. I figured you had the bags. Where were you?"

"I went to Warwick High School," Tom confessed, looking a little confused. "When I asked Courtney where the game was, she said, 'The high school gym.' So I went to my old gym at Warwick High by mistake. That's where Courtney and I used to go to high school. Isn't that funny?"

No one was laughing.

Poor Tom. It took him a while to notice everyone's panic. "Uh-oh, does this mean you might forfeit the game?" he asked.

"Not if I can help it," Tipper answered. "Now you and Buzz go outside. Tell the team to hurry to the locker room and change. They've only got a few minutes to get out on the court."

The national anthem was already playing when the Fast Breakers finally appeared in the gym. Some of the girls hadn't quite pulled up their socks. Some sneakers were untied. But each of the girls stood tall and faced the Blue Stars across the way.

The big game was about to begin.

The Fast Breakers lived up to their name. When the starting buzzer went off, Patsy tipped the ball to Jessie. A tall Blue Stars player stayed on Jessie like a shadow. Jessie remembered all her training with Tipper.

"Look, she's passing the ball to Violet!" Soo Lee said from the bleachers.

"It's Aldens all the way!" Henry shouted. He was proud that his sisters got the ball so early in the game.

Violet was surrounded by Blue Stars players. The Aldens could see that she was nervous.

"Good, she's passing the ball back to Patsy," Buzz said.

"Do you think Patsy is going to shoot now?" Henry asked Buzz.

"I hope not," Buzz answered. "She's too

far away. She should pass it to Mary Kate. She's a lot closer to the basket."

Though Patsy was some distance from the backboard, she seemed about to shoot. Then she caught a glimpse of Tipper on the sidelines.

"Great! She's passing it to Mary Kate, and . . . it's in!" Buzz screamed. "Mary Kate scored the first two points!"

"Go, girls!" Henry shouted out.

"The Blue Stars are fantastic, but they're all over the place," Buzz pointed out at half-time. The Fast Breakers were ahead by six points. "Tipper's girls are like a drill team. They know all their teammates' steps plus their own. Way to go!"

"Can we go down and see the team?" Benny asked Buzz.

"You bet," Buzz said. "Here, I'll help you get through the crowds."

Down on the court, Buzz, Soo Lee, and Benny waited until Tipper finished her half-time pep talk. "You girls just keep playing the second half like the first. I know the Blue Stars are rough and tough, but they're getting tired. If I know Courtney, she'll keep playing the same few players."

"I'm not tired at all," one of the Fast Breakers said.

"Neither am I," several of the other girls mumbled.

"Hey, Aldens, how do you think we're doing?" Tipper asked.

"Incredible!" Henry answered.

"You're the best ones," Benny answered. "Even though you were late."

The whole team laughed when they heard this.

"Well, we're not going to be late for the second half," Jessie said. "Wish us luck."

"Good luck!" Buzz and the Aldens yelled.

The huddle broke up. Buzz and the Aldens returned to the bleachers.

The second half began. The game was never even close.

"The Blue Stars look as if they're running through Jell-O," Buzz said when the game was in the final minutes.

Soo Lee pulled Buzz's arm. "I don't see any Jell-O."

Mr. Alden and Henry laughed.

"They have rubber legs," Buzz explained to the little girl.

This made Soo Lee even more confused.

Benny knew what Buzz meant. "You know how when we get tired, we get floppy legs, Soo Lee? Like that."

"The Blue Stars are tired," Henry said. "Courtney doesn't rotate players the way Tipper does. So even their good players are making a lot of mistakes."

Henry was right. As the second half of the game went on, the Blue Stars made more mistakes than baskets. The Fast Breakers were on a streak. By the time the final buzzer went off, the score was 32–22. The Fast Breakers fans broke into a roar.

"Look, Soo Lee!" Benny said, pointing to the Fast Breakers down on the court. "The Fast Breakers have rubber legs, too. They're jumping up and down like rubber balls!"

"You were the best, Jessie," Benny said when everybody went down to congratulate the team.

"And you were the best," Soo Lee told Violet.

"The team was the best!" Buzz told his sister. "It was almost like those old Greenfield-Warwick games. They were great, but you girls were even better. Congratulations, everybody. Now go out on the court. The mayor is going to present your trophy."

The Fast Breakers stood straight and tall in a line in the middle of the basketball court. Flashbulbs went off all over the gym as proud parents and friends snapped picture after picture of the winning team.

Everyone quieted down when they heard the scratchy sound of a microphone.

"I am pleased to present the league trophy to the coach of the Fast Breakers, Tipper Nettleton," the mayor announced to the excited fans.

Tipper waved and smiled at the crowd. The mayor handed her the league trophy in one hand and the microphone in the other.

Tipper waited for the crowd to quiet down again. She looked at the crowd and held up the trophy. "I'm going to hand this over to my players to hold one by one. This league trophy doesn't belong to me, but to each of the Fast Breakers. They're a great team."

With that, Tipper gave the trophy to the first girl in the Fast Breakers lineup, who passed it to the next girl. The crowd applauded loudly as each girl held it up for the crowd.

The trophy reached Patsy Cutter, who was the last girl in line. But Patsy wouldn't take it. Finally the other girl gave up and handed the trophy to Tipper instead.

When the team went to the locker room to change, Patsy just got her things and left. Why wasn't she staying and celebrating with her teammates? In the excitement of their victory, the girls forgot about Patsy and just kept hugging and cheering. They were the champs!

CHAPTER 10

Lost and Found

That afternoon, there were two trophies on the Aldens' mantel. Mr. Alden took pictures of Henry, Jessie, and Violet standing with the twins in front of the fireplace. No one wanted to spoil the moment by mentioning that there were supposed to be three trophies in the picture.

"My lips ache," Tipper said after everyone had finished posing. "I've never smiled so much in one day as I did today."

"Same here," said Buzz. "But save a few smiles for Great-Aunt Nora. We promised

to be at her house in fifteen minutes. Let's
go."

The Aldens followed the twins out to
their car. The twins were going to visit
some relatives for a couple of nights.

"So long, everyone," Tipper said. "See
you on Opening Day, trophy or no trophy."

"Wait a moment," Mr. Alden called out
when he noticed a letter for Tipper in the
mailbox. "Here's a letter for you."

"What an odd envelope." Tipper tore it
open. "It's written in big block letters
without a return address." She unfolded
the sheet of notebook paper inside. "Goodness!" she cried. "Listen:

" '*Your trophy is safe. You will find it at the
sports center on Opening Day.*' "

Tipper's face grew pale. "Do you know
anything about this?" she asked Buzz.

"Why are you asking me?" Buzz wanted
to know. He started the car up. "Let's not
talk about this now. I don't want to ruin our
visit with Great-Aunt Nora."

"Leave the note with us," Jessie whispered. "Maybe we can figure it out."

Tipper gave Jessie the note. After the twins drove off, Soo Lee and Benny held the piece of paper up to the sunlight.

"No fingerprints," Benny said. "But know what? If we find out who writes like this, maybe we can find Tipper's missing trophy."

Soo Lee didn't mean to giggle, but she couldn't help it. "I write in big letters! But I don't know all my letters yet."

The Aldens laughed over this, though Tipper's missing trophy was no laughing matter.

The Aldens spent the next day decorating the sports center with balloons and streamers. They made signs showing where the celebrations were going to be. They set up the tables and chairs for refreshments. And the whole time they worked, they kept their eyes open for Tipper's trophy.

"I just went into Mr. Fowler's office to ask about the folding chairs," Henry told Jessie and Violet when he saw them putting up posters on a bulletin board.

"While Henry was talking, Soo Lee and I peeked on his desk," Benny whispered. "But we didn't see any pieces of paper like Tipper's letter."

"He writes with eensy-weensy letters," Soo Lee added. "Not big, giant letters. We peeked in the closet, too, but there were only old paint cans in there."

Jessie smiled. "Good work, you two. I just hope whoever wrote that note is right — that the trophy will be here tomorrow. But I sure would like to find it ahead of time."

"Hey, Aldens," the children heard Tom Hooper call out when he saw them. He set a messy stack of papers on the floor. "Here, use some double-sided tape, Jessie. That works better than plain tape for putting up signs."

While Tom helped Jessie, Soo Lee and Benny pretended to pick up something from the floor.

"Thanks," Tom said when he saw Benny and Soo Lee gathering up his papers. "So long, now. Just throw the tape in my toolbox when you're done, Jessie. It's in the office closet with my painting gear."

"Tom didn't have any paper like that note," Benny whispered after Tom left. "And he has little bitsy handwriting, too."

When the Aldens went to the office, Courtney was talking on the phone.

Jessie held up the roll of tape. "Don't hang up. We're just putting this back in Tom's toolbox."

By this time Courtney had hung up the phone. "Fine, just shut the office door when you leave. And don't touch anything on this desk."

So they didn't. Instead, Benny and Soo Lee tried to see if any paper on Courtney's desk matched the paper the mystery writer had used.

"Nope," Benny said, looking over but not touching anything.

Outside, a cleaning person was pushing a cart down the hall.

"Look what fell off." Henry picked up a sheet of paper with red marker letters on

top. "It's an old practice schedule for the Blazers. It says, '*Give to Buzz.*' "

Jessie looked over Henry's shoulder. "It's the schedule Buzz was supposed to get for the first practice. I guess Mr. Fowler forgot to give it to Buzz. Maybe the mix-up wasn't on —"

"On purpose!" the Aldens heard Mr. Fowler say. "So that's what everybody thinks? That I made things hard for Buzz Nettleton?"

The Aldens didn't speak. They *did* believe Mr. Fowler made things hard for Buzz on purpose.

"Everybody's wrong thinking I'm out to get Buzz. I had the record for ten years before he broke it. I knew somebody was going to break my record someday."

By this time Courtney had come out to see what the commotion was all about. She overheard Frank getting upset. "You know what's hard?" she asked, looking at the Aldens. "That everything Frank and I did was pushed aside just because the Nettleton twins came back. Frank and I worked with the neighborhood teams for months. Then the twins showed up. Pretty soon all we were good for was making up schedules and such."

"The twins are leaving in a couple of days," Mr. Fowler said. "But we'll still be here. Only there aren't any newspapers and television people looking to talk to us."

The Aldens felt awful. Frank Fowler and Courtney Post had worked hard with the teams.

"What about our game?" Henry asked. "It seemed like you wanted the Blazers to lose just because Buzz was coaching us."

Mr. Fowler was quiet now. "I'll admit I made a lot of bad calls during the game. I should have let Tom referee the game, but he can get so distracted. He even forgot to give Buzz this schedule change. Not to mention the mix-up with the television people I found out about. Tom took the message from them but forgot to tell the twins about it. So the crew showed up at the sports center and no one was there."

Henry still wanted to know what happened at the Blazers game. "Were you upset with our team?"

"In a way I was," Mr. Fowler said. "I let my own jealousy get me in a bad mood. I guess I took it out on your team. For sure, I wasn't thinking straight during that game. I'm sorry about that. But, hey, guess what?"

"The Blazers won the trophy anyway!" Henry said proudly. "Speaking of trophies . . ."

Courtney shrugged her shoulders. "Hey, don't look at me. I'm sorry about what happened at our first practice. I found Tipper's keys and kept them. I . . . well . . . I was afraid the team would like her better than they liked me. I tried to make her look disorganized in front of the girls. But I didn't have anything to do with that missing trophy. I still have one more year of college. I'd rather win my own trophy than take it from Tipper. She's taught me a lot about how to be a good team player. Maybe next year I'll be the Most Valuable Player!"

The next day, the Aldens dressed up in their basketball uniforms. Mr. Alden whistled while he put on his most colorful bow tie.

"Why such long faces?" he asked when he noticed no one else seemed very excited about Opening Day. "I know you're wondering about that trophy. But we must trust the writer of that letter and hope for the best. Now let's head out. We don't want to be late!"

The parking lot was packed when Mr. Alden drove up to the sports center. People were streaming into the brand-new building. There were balloons inside the lobby. The Aldens could hear the Greenfield High School band playing inside the gym.

"Your decorations look very fine," Mr. Alden told his grandchildren. "I see Nora Nettleton going in. The twins must be here already. I'll meet you all in the front row of the gym. I'll be with the twins and some of their Greenfield relatives and friends."

Soo Lee tugged Jessie's sleeve. "I forgot to brush my hair."

"Me, too." Benny tried to flatten a curl of hair that just wouldn't stay down.

Jessie took the younger children by the hand. "I'll bring you both to the locker room so you can get nice and spiffy. But first, Benny, take this envelope to the referee. Patsy wrote up the team's names, numbers, and records for the game."

Benny took the envelope from Jessie. He tried to read the words. "Fast Breakers Statis . . . What's this hard word?" Before Jessie could answer, Benny noticed something else. "Hey! Look at the letters on this envelope! Where's that note about the missing trophy? I think the letters are the same!"

Jessie reached into her gym bag. She pulled out the crumpled note and smoothed it out.

"Look. It's the same printing as on this envelope!" Benny cried.

"I bet if we find Patsy, we'll find Tipper's trophy," Jessie said.

"I saw Patsy go up that staircase about ten minutes ago," Henry said when he overheard the children talking. "There's another locker room on the second floor."

Soo Lee and Benny raced up the stairs with Jessie and Henry following right behind.

The halls leading to the locker room were dark. But Jessie knew the way. She pushed open the door and searched for the light switch. But she couldn't find it. The children followed her into the darkened room.

The Aldens were not alone. They stood still. There was just enough light to see someone standing in front of a large wall mirror — someone holding a tall, silver trophy!

"Patsy!" Jessie cried out.

Patsy jumped when she saw the Aldens' reflection. She quickly put the trophy under one of the benches.

"Where did you find that?" Violet asked.

Patsy didn't answer.

"We've been searching for that ever since it disappeared," Henry said.

"I'm the one who took it from the trunk of the twins' car after I saw Buzz put it there," Patsy told Henry.

"Why?" Jessie asked, her voice shaking.

Patsy took a deep breath. "I just wanted to have it overnight — without anyone around. I tried to get it back to your room, Jessie. But you kept following me."

Jessie picked up the trophy from under the bench.

"I saw Tipper on television when she won it last month," Patsy continued. "I couldn't believe she was actually in Greenfield coaching our team. I thought if I borrowed her trophy, some of her talent might rub off on me. I want to be a great player like her — and Courtney, too."

"Why didn't you tell her?" Soo Lee asked.

Patsy went on, "I tried to get it back to her, but it was never the right time. Then, when our team won the league trophy, I felt worse. Tipper helped us win it, and I had taken hers. So I sent her the note and planned to bring it back today without getting caught."

"Well, here it is!" Jessie said. "We'd better bring it to the gym right away. Tipper would be pretty embarrassed if the mayor called her to the gym floor and she was empty-handed. You can tell her the whole story later."

Soo Lee forgot all about brushing her hair. Benny forgot about the curl that wouldn't behave. None of it mattered.

When the Aldens walked into the gym with Patsy, they held up the trophy so Tipper could see it. The spotlights made the silver reflect all over the gym. Tipper gave Patsy and the Aldens a thumbs-up sign.

When Patsy and the Aldens entered the gym, the band was playing the Greenfield High School fight song. Cheerleaders were tumbling and doing somersaults in front of the crowd.

The mayor tapped the microphone, which made a horrible scratchy sound. "Ladies and gentlemen," the mayor said, "may I present Tipper Nettleton, the Most Valuable Player in the country. She will now donate her trophy to our new sports center."

Jessie handed Benny the trophy. "Go ahead. Take it down to her."

Benny ran down to the gym floor. He held up the trophy. The mayor gave him the microphone. In a voice just like the mayor's, Benny said, "May I present Tipper Nettleton with the most valuable trophy that was ever missing."

All of the Aldens laughed, and the whole audience joined in. Benny laughed harder than anyone.

THE SPY IN THE BLEACHERS

created by

GERTRUDE CHANDLER WARNER

Illustrated by Robert Papp

ALBERT WHITMAN & Company
Chicago, Illinois

Library of Congress Cataloging-in-Publication Data
is available from the Library of Congress.

The Spy in the Bleachers
Created by Gertrude Chandler Warner;
Illustrated by Robert Papp.

ISBN: 978-0-8075-7606-9 (hardcover)
ISBN: 978-0-8075-7607-6 (paperback)

10 9 8 7 6 5 4 3 2 1 LB 14 13 12 11 10

Cover art by Robert Papp.

For information about Albert Whitman & Company,
visit our web site at www.albertwhitman.com.

Contents

CHAPTER I

Cogwheel Stadium

"Wow!" said Benny. "Two baseball fields! One is on the outside, and another one's on the inside." Benny was six years old. He was excited that Grandfather was taking them to a baseball stadium. Not just for a day, but for a whole week!

Jessie, who was twelve, smiled at her younger brother. "There's nobody using the outdoor ball field right now," she said. "What does that make you think?" All four Alden children were good at solving mysteries, but

Jessie was the one who always listed the facts and what they meant.

"It makes me think we can use it right now," said Benny eagerly.

"Or, it makes me think we aren't allowed to use it," said ten-year-old Violet. She was the shyest of the Aldens. As she spoke she slipped a baseball glove onto her left hand.

"Who's right?" kidded Henry. "Benny or Violet?" Henry was fourteen and very good at figuring out how things worked. Sometimes he even invented his own tools. This time he said, "Look at the sign."

Grandfather parked the car in the big parking lot surrounding Cogwheel Stadium. They would stay at an inn here in the town of Clayton. And they would go to a baseball game every day.

The four Alden children lived with their grandfather, James Alden. After their parents had died, the children had run away from home and lived in the woods in an old boxcar. They had never met their grandfather and thought he would be mean. But their grandfather found them and they learned he was a good person.

All five Aldens climbed out of the car and looked at the sign. *Play Ball!* the sign said. *Whenever You Want To.*

"Benny is right," said Violet happily. "We can use the ball field!"

"After you're done," said Grandfather, "go to the front gate of the stadium. Tell them that Jim Tanaka left tickets for you."

Grandfather walked toward the front gate of Cogwheel Stadium. Henry, Jessie, Violet, and Benny took bats and balls and gloves onto the field.

"Jessie can pitch," said Henry, "and I'll catch. Violet and Benny can take turns hitting."

Violet turned to Benny. "You can bat first, and I'll try to catch what you hit. Then we can switch places."

Benny stood at the plate and Jessie threw the ball. Benny took a wide swing with the bat. He missed the ball.

"Watch the ball as it leaves Jessie's hand,"

Henry told him. "Just keep your eye on the ball, then hit it."

Benny watched the ball. When it came to him, he swung his bat. The bat hit the ball and the ball bounced across the infield. Violet ran to pick it up near first base.

"Good one," said Henry.

After Jessie threw twenty pitches to Benny, it was Violet's turn to bat.

Benny stood near second base and watched. He saw Henry had his catcher's mitt pointed down. His other hand was down, too. Henry was moving his fingers up and down, almost like he was counting. Benny saw one finger down, then two fingers down, then three fingers down. Then back to one finger.

"Hey!" said Benny. "What's Henry doing with his fingers?"

Jessie turned around to answer. "I want to practice my pitching, so Henry is giving me signs on what to throw."

"Signs?" asked Benny. "What kind of signs?"

"Signs with his fingers. One finger down

is a sign that he wants me to throw a fastball. Two fingers down is a sign that he wants me to throw a change-up."

"What's a change-up?" asked Benny.

"It looks just like a fastball, but comes in slower."

Benny thought about this. "When I watched the ball come out of your hand, sometimes it came fast. But sometimes I swung before the ball even got to me. That pitch must have been a change-up!"

"That's right," said Jessie. "If you had known the pitch was going to be a change-up, you would have been ready for it. You would have hit the ball." Jessie turned back to throw to Violet.

By now the parking lot was half full. The Aldens gathered their balls, bats, and gloves and put them in the car.

They four of them walked to the front gate of Cogwheel Stadium. "Look at the long line of cars waiting to park," said Violet.

"That's part of the reason Grandfather is here," Jessie reminded her. "So many people are coming to Cogwheel Stadium that Grandfather is going to help with plans to make the stadium bigger. It needs more parking spaces. And more seats."

When they reached the turnstile, Henry spoke to the man taking tickets. "We're the Aldens. Our grandfather told us that Mr. Jim Tanaka left tickets for us."

"Welcome," said the man as he let them through the turnstiles. "*I'm* Jim Tanaka, and here are your four tickets." He reached into his shirt pocket and pulled out the tickets.

"Thank you," said Jessie. "Do all baseball team owners stand at the front gate?"

Jim Tanaka laughed. "Not usually," he said. "I'm here because the stadium is so crowded we don't have enough help."

"We'll help," said Henry. "We're very good at helping."

"Oh, I couldn't ask you to help," said Mr. Tanaka. "You're my guests, and you're here to enjoy the game."

"But we enjoy helping," said Jessie. "Especially if our help is needed."

"I really do need help," Mr. Tanaka said. "Thank you for asking. You can start—Oh, hello."

Benny turned to see who Mr. Tanaka was talking to. It was a man dressed in shorts and a flowered shirt. He wore a Cogs baseball cap and sunglasses. The cap brim was pulled down so low that it hid the man's face. In his hand was a pencil and small notebook.

Instead of saying hello, the man raised a finger to his lips and whispered, "Shhhh!"

"Oh," said Jim Tanaka. "Right." He let the man through the turnstiles.

"Who was that?" asked Benny.

"Oh, uh, nobody," answered Jim Tanaka. "Now let me show you what you'll be doing." He looked at the children again. "Henry and Violet, I'm going to put you here, at the front gate, just behind the ticket takers."

He walked over to a large cardboard box and reached in. He pulled out something large and orange. "These are today's giveaways," Mr. Tanaka explained. "I want you to give one to each person who comes in."

"This is great," said Henry. "It's a foam glove shaped like a cog!" Henry put a hand into a glove and waved it around.

"The fans love these free gloves," Mr. Tanaka said. "When the Cogs are winning, everybody wears a glove and waves it in the air."

Benny could see that the word *Cogs* was written on the orange shape. "What's a cog?" he asked.

"A cog is a gear," Mr. Tanaka answered. "It's a circle made out of metal. Old cogs used to be made out of wood."

Benny looked at the foam shape. "What are all those bumps sticking out around the cog?"

"Those are called teeth," Henry explained. "If you put two gears together, the teeth of one slide into the spaces of the other. That way, one gear turns the other gear."

"Like on our bikes!" said Benny excitedly.

"That's right," said Mr. Tanaka. "Many, many years ago the town of Clayton was a cog-making center. That's why my team is called the Clayton Cogwheels. 'Cogs' for short."

Mr. Tanaka spoke to Jessie and Benny. "We'll leave Henry and Violet here to hand out foam gloves. The two of you follow me, please. I'll take you to where you can help."

Henry and Violet watched Jessie, Benny, and Mr. Tanaka walk through the crowd. Then they began to give out free foam gloves as the fans came through the turnstile.

"Oh, thank you!" said one fan. "My son and daughter love the Cogs." Violet watched the mother, son, and daughter each put on a Cogs glove and wiggle it.

"This is fantastic!" another fan said to Henry. "The Cogs finished first last year. And it looks like they'll win the pennant again this year."

"That's for sure," said the next fan in line. "Only five games left to go, all of them here in Cogwheel Stadium."

Violet knew that was good news. When a team played on their home field, they had a better chance of winning.

"How many games do the Cogs have to win in order to win the pennant?" she asked Henry.

"Only two," Henry answered. "If the Cogs win two of these last five games, they win the pennant."

"The Cogs aren't going to win two of the last five games," called out a young man who had overheard them. He wore a Hatters baseball cap. "The Hatters will win all five and win the pennant. Go, Hatters!" he shouted as he walked by.

"Look at all the Hatters baseball caps coming our way," whispered Henry. "There are as many Hatters fans here as there are Cogs fans."

A young woman taking tickets at the turnstile smiled at Henry and Violet. "The Hatters are from Madison, which is the next town over. The Hatters and Cogs have been rivals for over a century."

"Wow!" breathed Henry. "These should be very exciting games!"

Violet watched a young woman come

through the turnstile. The woman had long blonde hair that she wore in braids. She was dressed in a white T-shirt, denim shorts, and white sneakers. Was she a Cogs fan or a Hatters fan? She wore a visor instead of a cap. The visor didn't say anything. Around her neck the young woman had a pair of binoculars.

Violet held out a free glove.

The woman took the foam glove from Violet and tore it in half. Then she threw the two halves on the ground and stomped on them. "I hate the Cogs!" she shouted. "They're a rotten, no-good team! I hope that Cody Howard hits four home runs! I hope the Cogs lose every one of the five games!" The woman stomped away, into the crowd.

"Whoa!" said Henry. "She's a Hatters fan, for sure."

Violet picked up the two halves of the foam glove and threw them into a trash barrel. "Who's Cody Howard?" she asked her brother.

"He plays center field for the Hatters,"

Henry answered. "He's a great hitter. He might win the league batting title this year." Henry explained to Violet that each year the batting title was won by the player who had the highest batting average.

"Does that mean the player who has the most hits in a season?" asked Violet.

"Yes," answered Henry.

"Whoever wins the batting title wins a brand new car," said a man with a Cogs baseball cap. "I hope it's not Cody Howard," he said.

"Because he's a Hatter?" Henry asked the fan.

"Yeah," answered the fan. "I'd like to see the Cogs catcher, Reese Dawkins, win the title and the car."

Henry and Violet handed out free foam gloves until there weren't any left.

CHAPTER 2

View from the Bleachers

While Henry and Violet were giving out free gloves, Jessie and Benny followed Mr. Tanaka. Thousands of fans crowded the open area inside the stadium. Jessie saw that the fans were buying pennants and T-shirts and caps. Benny saw that the fans were buying food: hot dogs and popcorn and ice cream.

They followed Mr. Tanaka through an unmarked door. Now they stood inside a very large kitchen. Men and women in white aprons were cooking hundreds of hot dogs on grills. Others were putting the dogs into buns and wrapping them in clean paper. Still others were filling large paper boxes full of popcorn.

"This is a very busy place," Jessie said. "Everybody is working hard."

"Yes," replied Mr. Tanaka. "Cogs fans are hungry fans."

Benny stood still, staring at all the food.

Jim Tanaka looked down at him. "I'll bet you're hungry," he said.

Benny looked up. "How did you know?" he asked.

"I have a grandson your age," said Mr. Tanaka. "He's always hungry." Mr. Tanaka grabbed two large boxes of popcorn off a counter. He handed one to Jessie and one to Benny. "Eat some popcorn," he said, "and follow me around this room. I'll explain how you can help."

"Thank you," said Jessie as she took her box of popcorn.

"Thank you," said Benny. He shoved a

large handful of popcorn into his mouth. "Yum," he said.

Mr. Tanaka pointed to a metal door, not the one they had come through. "See all the vendors coming through that door?" he asked. Then he looked down at Benny. "A vendor is somebody who sells things."

"Like popcorn," said Benny, eating another large handful.

"Yes," answered Mr. Tanaka. "Some vendors sell food. Others sell baseball caps or pennants."

"Souvenirs," said Jessie.

"That's right," said Mr. Tanaka. He looked at them. "Would you rather help with the food or the souvenirs?"

"The food!" answered Benny right away.

Jim Tanaka laughed. "I thought so. Follow me."

Jessie and Benny followed him to one side of the large kitchen. Workers were putting just-cooked hot dogs in paper wrappers.

"Jessie, do you think you can wrap these hot dogs and stack them inside these vendor boxes?" asked Mr. Tanaka.

"Yes," said Jessie. "I can do a good job at that." She began to wrap and stack hot dogs.

"Very good," Mr. Tanaka said. "I really appreciate your help."

"You're welcome," said Jessie. In no time at all, she had filled one vendor box. As soon as she closed the lid on the box somebody took it from her. It was a young man.

"Hello, Carlos," Mr. Tanaka said to him. "I'd like you to meet Jessie Alden and her brother Benny. They volunteered to help us out today. Jessie and Benny, this is Carlos Garcia."

Jessie and Benny said hello to Carlos.

Benny stared at Carlos' baseball cap. A tall stiff wire stood up at the back of his cap, like an antenna. At the top of the wire was a Cogs pennant.

"Nice to meet you," said Carlos as he hurried away with a full box of hot dogs.

"Carlos is one of our best vendors," Mr. Tanaka said. "He works the bleachers, right where you'll be sitting."

"We'll buy our hot dogs from Carlos, then," said Jessie.

"Carlos will be easy for you to find," said Mr. Tanaka. "He wears that tall wire and pennant just so hungry fans can spot him. I sit in the owner's box near home plate—even I can see Carlos in the bleachers."

Before he left, Mr. Tanaka showed Benny how to load trays with boxes of popcorn. Benny liked this job.

Jessie loaded more boxes with hot dogs. Soon Carlos Garcia was back.

"You sell your hot dogs really fast," Jessie said.

Carlos laughed. "I'm a very good vendor," said Carlos. "But I'm an even better catcher." He frowned. "Better than Reese Dawkins, that's for sure."

"Who's Reese Dawkins?" asked Jessie.

"He's the Cogs catcher," explained Carlos. "And he doesn't know which pitches to call." Carlos picked up a full box of hot dogs and left.

Jessie was happy that she was able to help

Mr. Tanaka. Helping other people felt good. Soon one of the cooks came up to Jessie and Benny. "Thank you," he said. "Now you can go enjoy the game."

Jessie and Benny hurried out the door. Once again they were in the middle of thousands of fans. The two of them walked slowly, moving between groups of people.

They almost walked into the back of a large, fuzzy, orange circle. It was taller than Jessie. It had two legs that stuck out of the bottom. It had two arms which stuck out of the sides. It was a person in a big, strange costume!

"What's that?" asked Benny. "It has those things sticking out of it. Teeth, that's what they're called."

"Yes," said Jessie. "It looks like a giant walking cog. I'll bet it's the team mascot." Jessie had seen other sports mascots. They were people who wore big, fuzzy costumes.

Suddenly a group of children older than Benny ran up to the giant walking cog. "Wheelie!" they shouted, "Wheelie!" The cog turned around and around, bowing to the children.

Jessie saw words written across the front of the costume: *Wheelie the Cogwheel.*

As Benny and Jessie watched, Wheelie did a little dance for the children. Then he bowed to them again and continued walking.

"Let's stay behind Wheelie," said Benny. "I like to watch him."

Benny watched the fans. They held things out to Wheelie—napkins, pieces of paper, baseballs, and caps. One of them gave Wheelie a pen and the mascot autographed a napkin. After he autographed the napkin, the mascot held out a hand. The fan walked away.

Next Wheelie autographed a baseball. Once again he held out his hand. Benny saw the man with the autographed baseball put money into Wheelie's hand. Quickly, Wheelie's hand disappeared into his costume. Then it came out again, empty.

Just as Benny was about to tell Jessie what he saw, he heard cheering. Wheelie was racing down the aisle toward the playing field. Everyone was clapping and cheering to watch Wheelie run.

"Look," said Jessie, staring at the aisle number. "This is our section."

Jessie and Benny walked down the aisle, looking at row numbers. "I think we're way at the bottom," said Jessie. "We'll be very close to the baseball field." She was excited.

"I see Henry and Violet!" shouted Benny. He pointed to the second row of seats, where Henry and Violet sat.

"We just got here," Violet told Jessie and Benny. "We handed out all the foam gloves."

"I filled trays with popcorn boxes," Benny answered. "I could hardly keep up!"

"And I wrapped hot dogs and put them into vendor boxes," answered Jessie.

"I'm hungry," said Benny, looking around.

"Me, too," said Henry. "It's way past lunch time."

Jessie looked around, then smiled. She had spotted a pennant that seemed to float in the air. But she could tell that it was attached to a wire, and the wire was attached to a baseball cap. "Carlos!" she shouted.

"Who are you calling?" asked Henry.

"Carlos Garcia," said Jessie. "He's a hot dog vendor."

In no time at all Carlos reached their seats. The children bought hot dogs. Henry paid for the hot dogs and also gave Carlos a tip.

"Thanks," said Carlos. He added the money to a large stack of bills in his hand.

Henry noticed that the top of the stack had one-dollar bills. He thought he saw a hundred-dollar bill on the bottom. *If that's a hundred*, thought Henry, *somebody bought a lot of hot dogs!*

The children ate their hot dogs and looked all around.

Henry looked at the baseball field and the players. He could see home plate clearly. He would have a great view of each pitch as it crossed the plate.

Jessie looked for Wheelie. At last she spotted him. The mascot was so close! The first row, right in front of them, was filled

with fans. Wheelie was sitting just past the fans. His chair was on a long platform built just below the front row of seats. Jessie thought that the mascot had the best view in all of Cogwheel Stadium.

Violet was looking around at all the people. Many of them wore Cogs baseball caps. But almost as many wore Hatters baseball caps. Violet looked at her own baseball glove, which she had brought into the stadium. She would love to catch a home run ball. After Violet finished eating her hot dog, she slipped off her free Cogs glove and put it beside her. She put on her real baseball glove. Shyly, she kept her gloved hand on her lap, where nobody could see it.

Benny wanted to look everywhere! He wanted to see the baseball players. He wanted to see Wheelie. He wanted to see and hear all the people. And he wanted to keep Carlos and the hot dogs in sight.

"Can you see?" Henry asked his brother.

"I can see everything," said Benny. "At first I thought these seats were too far away, but now I like them."

The person in front of Benny turned around and smiled at him. "Bleacher seats are the best seats in the whole park," she told him. "From the bleachers you have the best view of the whole game. Especially home plate." She looked at Violet. "And in the bleachers you might be able to catch a home run ball!"

Violet looked at Henry, and Henry looked at Violet. They both recognized the young woman. She was the one who had torn the free glove in half and then stomped on it. Henry was surprised that she seemed such a happy, friendly person. He was even more surprised that she was wearing a Cogs baseball cap!

"I'm Henry Alden," he told her. "These are my sisters, Violet and Jessie, and my brother Benny. We're from Greenfield. This is our first time at Cogwheel Stadium."

"I'm Emma Larke," the young woman said. "Clayton is my home town."

"Are you a Cogs fan?" asked Violet, staring at Emma's baseball cap.

"I was," she answered. "I was a Cogs fan from the time I was five years old. But now I hate the Cogs," she said with a frown. "Especially Reese Dawkins, who's a horrible catcher."

Benny was confused. "But you're wearing a Cogs baseball cap," he said to Emma.

"Oh," she said, touching the brim of her cap. "I forgot." She took the cap off and put it in her canvas bag. Then she put a visor on and turned to face the field.

"Carlos Garcia doesn't like Reese Dawkins, either," Jessie told Henry and Violet. "He said so when I was loading hot dogs into his vendor box."

The Hatters batted first. Emma Larke jumped up and cheered every Hatter. The Cogs' pitcher struck out two of them. The third one grounded out to first.

Each time a Hatter made an out, Wheelie stood up and pumped his fists.

"The Cogs look like a good team," Jessie said.

The Cogs weren't able to score in the first

inning. Emma stood up and cheered each time a Cogs batter made an out.

"Hey, you!" yelled a fan several rows back. "Sit down!"

Between innings, Wheelie stood up and entertained the fans. First he puffed out his chest and strode back and forth on the platform. Then he pointed to the Hatters dugout and pinched his nose together with two fingers. Cogs fans cheered because Wheelie was telling them that the Hatters stank.

In the top of the second inning Cody Howard came to bat for the Hatters. Henry noticed that Cody batted left-handed, and the Cogs pitcher threw right-handed. Left-handed batters usually did well against right-handed pitchers.

Wheelie held his nose.

Emma stood up. She took off her visor and waved it in the air. "Go, Cody!" she shouted.

The pitch came in and Cody Howard blasted the ball into the bleachers. The home run sailed over their heads.

"Wow," said Jessie, "he guessed right on that pitch."

"Yes," said Henry. "It was a fastball."

The score was now 0-1. The Hatters were winning.

The next two Hatter players struck out swinging. Each time, Wheelie stood up and pretended to faint, as if their swings knocked him down.

Benny was having a great time. He loved seeing everything that was happening. He saw Carlos come down the aisle with two hot dogs in his hand. Carlos leaned over the rail and gave the two hot dogs to Wheelie.

Violet was also watching Carlos Garcia. She loved the way his orange Cogs pennant swayed on its wire. She saw Carlos take an envelope out of his pocket and give it to Wheelie. Carlos was frowning as he walked back up the aisle.

Jessie watched the game closely. From where she was sitting, she had a perfect view of the catcher. She could see Reese Dawkins put down one finger, then two, then three.

Although the Cogs got runners on base, they didn't score. At the top of the fifth inning, Cody Howard came to bat again.

Emma Larke stood up. She took her visor off, then put it on backwards. "Go, Cody!" she shouted again.

Wheelie stood up and stretched. He held his hand to his mouth like he was yawning. He sat back down.

Carlos stood at the railing behind Wheelie. He opened his metal vendor's box. He slammed its lid up and down three times.

The Cogs pitcher threw the ball and Cody Howard hit it the length of the park! Violet saw the ball coming their way. Everybody stood up to catch it. Violet saw the ball getting closer and closer—she reached for it with her baseball glove.

Violet felt the baseball land in her glove. *I caught it!* she thought. *I caught it!*

"Great catch!" shouted Henry.

"Wow!" said Jessie, patting her sister on the back. "That was terrific."

All the fans cheered.

Violet smiled shyly. She looked at the beautiful white baseball she had caught, turning it around in her hands.

"Can I see it?" asked Benny.

"Sure," said Violet, handing the ball to Benny.

Emma Larke turned around. "That was a very nice catch!"

"Thank you!" said Violet.

"You were smart to bring your glove," Carlos told her. "A good ballplayer is always ready."

Then Carlos frowned. "That's a second home run for Cody. He hit it because Reese Dawkins called the wrong pitch."

"The pitcher threw a curveball," said Henry, who had been watching closely.

"That's right," said Carlos. "And Cody hit it out of the ballpark. The Hatters are now leading, two-nothing."

"What do you think the pitcher should have called?" asked Jessie.

"A change-up," said Carlos. "Reese Dawkins called the wrong pitch." He banged the lid to his hot dog box a couple of times and walked away.

Everybody sat down again.

"That was a great catch, Violet," said Henry. "What a great souvenir of Cogwheel Stadium."

Violet grinned. "I'm going to put the baseball on my bookshelf at home."

Henry looked at Jessie. "Cody Howard acted like he knew what pitch was coming."

Jessie nodded. She remembered what she'd told Benny about the way catchers made signals to pitchers. The batter of the other team wasn't supposed to know what those signals were—but did Cody Howard know?

"I hope this isn't what it looks like," Jessie said to Henry.

The Cogs players tried to score, but didn't. In the top of the eighth inning, Cody Howard came to bat again.

Emma Larke turned around. "Cody is going to win the batting championship," she told the Aldens. "And Reese Dawkins *isn't*!" She clapped her hands.

Cody stepped up to the plate, the Cogs pitcher threw the ball, and Cody Howard hit it out of Cogwheel Stadium.

"It is what it looks like," Henry said to Jessie quietly.

Jessie nodded. "Somebody is stealing the signs Reese Dawkins is giving the pitcher."

"And that somebody is signaling the signs to Cody Howard," said Henry.

At the end of nine innings, the Cogs lost, 0-3. Cody Howard scored all three of the Hatters' runs.

"This is bad," said Henry. "Unless the sign-stealing stops, the Cogs might lose all five games. That means they would lose the pennant."

CHAPTER 3

Next to the Dugout

The next morning Grandfather drove the children to Cogwheel Stadium. He parked in the same spot as before. "I'll bet you want to play more ball today," he said.

"Actually, we want to help Mr. Tanaka as much as we can," said Jessie. Last night after dinner she and Henry had told Benny and Violet about the sign stealing. Now all four children wanted to find out who was stealing Reese Dawkins's signs and signaling them to Cody Howard.

Grandfather led them to the owner's office on the upper level of Cogwheel Stadium.

"Good morning," said Jim Tanaka. "Did you enjoy yesterday's game, even though we lost?" he asked.

"Yes," said Benny. "I love the bleachers."

"We had a very good time," said Jessie. "Thank you so much for the tickets. And we would like to help you today, if you still need help."

"I would love more help," replied Mr. Tanaka. "Henry and Benny, Wheelie could use your help. And Jessie and Violet, I've got a job for you too."

* * * *

Wheelie the mascot had his own small dressing room. The man who played the mascot was dressed in cargo shorts, a T-shirt, and socks. "I'm Winn Winchell," he told Henry and Benny. "Call me Winn when I'm not in costume. When I'm in costume, call me Wheelie."

"You talk!" said Benny.

"Yep," said Winn. "I talk when I'm Winn.

I don't talk when I'm Wheelie."

"Why?" asked Benny.

"Because cogwheels don't talk, that's why," answered Winn. He took the bottom half of the orange Wheelie costume off its hook.

Henry watched Winn step into the bottom half of the costume. Henry saw suspenders hanging from it. He grabbed the suspenders and held them up for Winn.

"You're a quick learner," said Winn. He pulled the suspenders over his shoulders. "See that box in the corner?"

Henry and Benny looked where Winn was pointing.

"Those are rolled-up T-shirts," Winn told them. He handed Henry a large canvas bag. "Stuff as many of them in here as you can," he said. "When I go out on the field, you carry the bag and follow me. You hand me one T-shirt at a time, and I throw it to a fan. Got that?"

"Yes," said Henry. *This is cool*, he thought. *I get to walk on the baseball field!*

Winn handed Benny a canvas bag, too.

"Plastic water bottles," he said. "You carry this bag and follow behind Henry. Sometimes I give away shirts, and sometimes I give away bottles."

"Now listen carefully," he told them. "Whenever we're out of T-shirts or water bottles, you let me know. That's when we come back here and take a break. And as soon as we get back here, you help me take off the top half of my costume. And then you hand me a tall glass of ice water. Immediately." Winn pointed to a small refrigerator in the corner." He looked at Henry and Benny. "Any questions?"

Henry and Benny shook their heads.

"Good," said Winn, "because Wheelie doesn't talk." He took the top half of his Wheelie costume from its hook and began to slip it over his head.

Henry helped Winn, who became Wheelie. Wheelie turned in a circle, then faced the door. He made a come-with-me motion with his arm. Henry and Benny grabbed their canvas bags. They followed Wheelie onto the baseball field.

As soon as he walked onto the baseball field, Wheelie turned three cartwheels. The fans cheered.

Henry was surprised at how loud the crowd noise was. Really loud! *So this is what baseball players hear*, he thought.

Wheelie waved his arms to the fans and they shouted louder. Henry followed the mascot as he walked around the field, close to the stands. Each time Wheelie threw a free T-shirt into the crowd, Henry handed him another one. And when he threw a plastic water bottle, Benny ran up with his canvas bag of bottles.

When they were out of T-shirts they went back to the dressing room. Henry helped take off the top half of Wheelie's costume. Benny poured a glass of ice water and handed it to the mascot.

Winn drank the entire glass of water. He handed the empty glass to Benny. "It's hot inside this costume," he said. He reached into the bottom half of the costume and pulled out a bandana. An envelope fell out of the bandana onto the floor. Money fell out of the envelope and scattered everywhere.

Benny stooped to pick up the money. He saw one-hundred dollar bills!

"Don't touch that!" shouted Winn. He bent down and pushed Benny aside.

Benny didn't like being pushed. He thought Winn was rude.

Henry bent down behind Winn and picked up the envelope. The word Wheelie was handwritten on it, in big letters. The handwriting slanted toward the left.

"Is that the money you charge for an autograph?" Benny asked.

"Mind your own business," said Winn as he grabbed the envelope out of Henry's hand. Winn stuffed the money back into the envelope. Then he pushed the envelope down into his pockets.

Henry stood up and pulled a sheet of paper out of his pocket and held it out toward the mascot. "Could I have your autograph?" Henry asked.

Winn looked at the piece of paper. "I'll give you an autograph if you give me ten dollars."

"Oh," said Henry, taking back his paper. "Let me think about it."

Henry now knew that the mascot wanted ten dollars for an autograph. But the envelope had been full of one-hundred-dollar bills. The money in the envelope wasn't for autographs. *What is it for, then?* thought Henry. *And why did Winn get so upset about it?*

"Fill up your canvas bags," Winn told Henry and Benny. "We go out the door again in five minutes."

* * * *

Jessie and Violet were helping out in the large open area behind the bleachers. A small waterfall had been built there. Fans could walk into it and cool off on really hot days. Jessie and Violet helped the line of people move along. Violet kept the line straight and alongside the wall. Jessie let everybody have one minute under the waterfall, then it was the next person's turn.

"Time's up," said Jessie to a girl who was

about Benny's age.

"*Awww*," said the girl as she stepped out of the waterfall.

"You can get back in line and do it again," said Jessie with a smile. She watched as the girl ran to the back of the long line and stood there, dripping wet. There were other dripping wet people in line, too.

"It's so hot," said Violet. "I feel like walking through the waterfall myself, just to cool off."

"The waterfall is a wonderful idea," said Jessie. "Mr. Tanaka makes sure the fans have a lot of fun."

Violet nodded, then frowned. "I hope the Cogs win today. Maybe the sign stealer won't be here today."

Violet noticed a woman wearing a lavender dress. Violet loved all shades of purple and always noticed them. But she wondered why somebody would wear such a beautiful, dressy dress to a ballgame.

The woman had long blonde hair that curled up at the ends. She wore a straw hat with a wide brim.

The woman turned around. It was Emma Larke.

Emma didn't notice Violet or Jessie or even the waterfall. She seemed to be looking around for something, or somebody.

"Look," Violet said to her sister. "It's Emma Larke. She looks so different from yesterday. Let's say hello."

But just then Carlos Garcia walked up to Emma. He didn't notice Jessie or Violet, either.

"Reese Dawkins looked bad yesterday," the sisters heard Carlos say to Emma.

"Yes, but he's still playing today," answered Emma.

"The manager doesn't want to switch catchers this late in the season," said Carlos. "But next year—next year will be different."

Emma opened her straw handbag and pulled out her binoculars. She showed them to Carlos.

As Emma was showing the binoculars to Carlos, Violet saw Carlos pull an envelope from his pocket. Violet noticed handwriting on the envelope, but she couldn't see what it said. She saw Carlos drop the envelope into Emma's purse.

Carlos turned and saw her. "Hello, Violet," he said. "What are you doing?"

"Hello," said Violet. "We're helping out with the waterfall shower."

Emma turned, too, and said hello to Violet and Jessie. "I would have gone into the waterfall yesterday," she said, "but I don't want to get my clothes wet today."

"That's a beautiful dress," said Violet.

Emma twirled around, to show off her dress. "Thank you," she said. Emma reached into her straw purse and pulled out a pair of white lace gloves. She put them on and wiggled her fingers. Then Emma and Carlos walked away from the waterfall.

Violet saw them talking as they left. She wondered about Emma's binoculars. She wondered even more about Emma's white lace gloves.

* * * *

All four children met up in the aisle and walked down to their seats.

"Mr. Tanaka has given us tickets in the very first row," Jessie said.

"Right next to the Cogs dugout," Henry pointed out.

Benny stopped just before they entered their row. "Look," he said.

Jessie, Violet, and Henry looked. There was one other person in their row. He was sitting right next to the Cogs dugout. He wore dark sunglasses and a Cogs baseball cap pulled low. He wore shorts and a flowered shirt, and he was writing something in a small notebook. It was the man who had entered the turnstile yesterday. He had whispered "*Shhh*" to Mr. Tanaka.

Henry led the way into the row and sat beside the man with the notebook. "Hello," said Henry. "I'm Henry Alden, and these are my sisters, Jessie and Violet, and my brother Benny."

"Pleased to meet you," said the man as he put away his notebook. "You look like a happy group. How did you get these great seats?"

"Mr. Tanaka gave them to us," answered Jessie.

The man nodded. "That's just like Jim Tanaka. Very generous. Are you friends of his?"

"Our grandfather is helping Mr. Tanaka expand the seating and parking for Cogwheel Stadium," said Henry.

"And we're helping Mr. Tanaka, too," said Benny. "Today Henry and I helped Wheelie."

"Aha!" said the man. "I thought the two of you looked familiar. You were on the field handing Wheelie T-shirts and water bottles." He pulled his notebook out of his shirt pocket. He wrote something in it quickly, then put it back into his pocket.

Jessie had been waiting for the man to introduce himself, but so far he hadn't. "What should we call you?" she asked him.

The man turned to look at them. That was when Henry noticed the small headphone the man was wearing. His baseball cap hid most of the headphone, but a small part could be seen.

"Do any of you like mysteries?" the man asked.

The children nodded. "We all like mysteries," Violet told him.

"Excellent," he replied. "Then you can call me 'Mr. X.' And now," he said, "the game is about to begin."

All four of the Aldens looked at Mr. X as he wrote something in his small notebook. Then he spoke softly into his headphone. Not even Henry, who was sitting right next to him, heard what he said.

The Cogs scored two runs in the bottom of the first inning. That made the Aldens very happy. That seemed to make Mr. X happy, too. He cheered the Cogs loudly.

Benny was starting to feel hungry. He wished Carlos Garcia were here to sell them hotdogs. Benny looked across the baseball field, into the bleachers. It didn't take him long to spot the tall pennant that Carlos wore on his head. "I can see Carlos!" he told Violet.

Violet looked in the direction Benny was

pointing. She saw Carlos give something to Wheelie. Probably a hot dog or a soft drink. She saw Emma Larke sitting in the front row of the bleachers. Emma's straw hat and lavender dress and white gloves made her very easy to see.

The second inning started. Cody Howard was the first man up for the Hatters. Henry tried to watch everything at once. He saw Wheelie hold his nose. He saw Emma Larke stand up and take off her straw hat. She waved it back and forth. Henry couldn't hear her from across the ballpark but he thought she must be shouting, "Go, Cody!"

Jessie was watching Carlos Garcia. When Cody came to bat, Carlos did not sell hot dogs. Carlos stood near the railing and watched Cody bat. She saw Carlos lift the lid of his vendor's box up and down.

The pitch came in and Cody Howard swung. Everybody heard a loud crack as the ball sailed out of Cogwheel Stadium.

"That proves it!" shouted a loud, angry voice. "Somebody is telling that batter what our pitching signals are! I want to know who is doing it!" Henry leaned over to see partway into the Cogs dugout. The person doing the shouting was Sam Jackson, the Cogs manager.

Mr. X spoke into his headphones and wrote something in his notebook.

"This is bad," Henry whispered to his sisters and brother. "We have to discover who is giving Cody Howard the Cogs' signals."

Jessie, Violet, and Benny nodded. Whoever was stealing signs was not a good sport.

The score remained Cogs 2, Hatters 1, until the top of the fifth inning, when Cody Howard hit another home run. The Hatters had a runner on, so now the Hatters were leading 3-2.

After Cody's second home run, Mr. X wrote for a long time in his notebook. Henry saw that Mr. X was right-handed.

Mr. X looked up from his notebook. "You kids say that you like mysteries," he said. "Well, here's a good mystery for you—there's a spy in the bleachers."

"A spy who is stealing Reese Dawkins' signs to the pitcher," said Jessie.

Mr. X looked surprised. "Say," he said, "you kids really are into mysteries, aren't you?"

The Aldens nodded.

"Well," said Mr. X, "I know who the spy is."

"You do?" asked Violet.

Mr. X nodded, then pointed across the baseball field into the bleachers. "It's the woman in the lavender dress," he said.

"How do you know she's the spy?" asked Violet.

"Obvious," said Mr. X. "She has binoculars so she can see the catcher's signs better. Then, each time Cody Howard is at bat, she stands up. She waves her visor or her straw hat or whatever she's wearing. That's how she signals Cody. Today she's wearing white lace gloves. Very suspicious, don't you think? So easy for the batter to see her hands."

In the bottom of the sixth inning, the Cogs scored two more runs to tie the score, 4-4.

But in the top of the seventh inning, Cody Howard came to bat again. Emma Larke stood up again and waved her straw hat. Cody did not hit a home run this time. But he did hit a triple, which allowed one of the Hatters already on base to score a run. The Hatters won the game, 5-4.

CHAPTER 4

In the Owner's Office

When the game was over, the children walked back to Mr. Tanaka's office.

Grandfather was there with Jim Tanaka, who looked very unhappy.

"Mr. Tanaka," said Henry. "The Cogs lost the last two games because somebody is stealing the catcher's signs."

"And that somebody is signaling the signs to Cody Howard," added Jessie. "That's why he hit five home runs and a triple in just two games. Because he knows. "

Mr. Tanaka rubbed his chin. "Well," he said slowly, "Cody Howard is a *very* good hitter. And he wants to win the batting title. Maybe that's why he hit all these home runs."

"It's true that Cody is a very good hitter," said Henry. "But he hit each of those home runs as if he knew *exactly* what pitch was coming."

Mr. Tanaka turned to Grandfather. "Your grandchildren are very, uh, unusual," he said.

"My grandchildren are very smart," said Grandfather. "They think things through. If they say somebody is stealing signs, they are most likely right."

"Hmmmm," said Mr. Tanaka, rubbing his chin again. "This is a very serious charge. Stealing signs is a very dirty trick."

Violet nodded. "It's not fair," she said.

"Hmmmm," Mr. Tanaka muttered again. He was about to reply, when the door opened with a bang.

Sam Jackson, the Cogs manager, burst into the office. "Somebody is stealing our signs!" he shouted. "That's why we lost these two games."

Before Mr. Tanaka could say anything, Wheelie came in just behind Sam. He was struggling to take off the top half of his costume. Sam Jackson turned around and helped him. "I told you this is none of your business," the manager said to the mascot.

"It *is* my business," replied Winn. "If somebody is stealing signs, I want to know who it is."

"*Your* job is to turn cartwheels," said Sam Jackson. "You stay out of this."

Mr. Tanaka raised a hand. "Quiet!" he said firmly.

The manager and the mascot stopped arguing.

"Sam," said Mr. Tanaka, "please continue with what you were saying."

"I tell you, somebody is stealing our signs! If we don't find out who it is and stop them, we're not going to win *any* of these five games. And you know we need to win *two games* to win the pennant." The manager looked at the Aldens. "What are these kids doing here?"

Mr. Tanaka introduced the children and Grandfather to Sam Jackson. "Henry, Jessie, Violet, and Benny have already told me about the sign stealing," he announced.

"What?" said Sam Jackson.

"Impossible!" said Winn.

"Not at all impossible," Grandfather replied. "My grandchildren have solved mysteries before."

Jessie explained why they thought someone was stealing the Cogs' signs and giving them to Cody Howard. Sam and Mr. Tanaka nodded their heads as Jessie talked.

But Winn shook his head. "There are ten thousand people out there," he said. "Even if there is a spy, how are you going to know who it is?"

Henry spoke. "We think there are only four suspects," he said.

"*Four?*" Winn held up four fingers and then pretended to faint.

Henry didn't like the way Winn was making fun of them. "We hope we can figure out which one is the spy during tomorrow's game," he told Mr. Tanaka.

"Who are these four suspects?" Sam Jackson demanded. "If what you say is true, let's keep all four of them out of the ballpark!"

"No, Sam, that's not right," replied Mr. Tanaka. "We would be keeping three innocent people away from the game."

"I don't care!" shouted the manager.

Mr. Tanaka looked at the Aldens. "Please," he said, "tell us who your four suspects are." "Three of them sit in the bleachers," said Benny, "and one sits right next to the Cogs dugout."

"*What?!*" said Mr. Tanaka, very upset. "No, that can't be."

Everybody waited for Mr. Tanaka to say something more, but he just stared at the top of his desk.

"The person who sits next to the Cogs dugout can't see the catcher's signs," Jessie said. "But he can hear what you're saying in the dugout," she told the manager. "And he's always writing in a small notebook."

"And he speaks into a headphone," added

Henry. "He might be talking to somebody who's somewhere else in the ballpark."

"Kick him out!" Sam Jackson shouted to Mr. Tanaka, who just shook his head.

"The three people in the bleachers can all see the catcher's signs," Henry explained. "And they all make motions that might be signals."

Sam Jackson lifted his baseball cap and rubbed his head again. "Tell me about these three. Who are they? What kind of motions do they make?"

Jessie told him about Emma Larke, one of the suspects. "Yesterday she wore a visor and stood up and waved it when Cody Howard came to bat. Today she wore a straw hat and did the same thing."

Violet told him about Carlos Garcia. "He's easy to see because his baseball cap has an antenna wire with a tall pennant at the top. Whenever Cody comes to bat, Carlos bangs the lid of his hot dog box."

"The third suspect is Wheelie the mascot," said Henry. "He sits in the best position to steal the signs. And every time Cody comes to bat, Wheelie holds his nose."

Sam Jackson looked at the children, then looked at Winn. "*Wheelie?*" he asked. "You can't be serious!"

Winn pretended to sob and wipe tears from his eyes.

"Cut it out, Winn." The manager was annoyed. "You kids are very observant. Based on what you've told me, it's obvious who the spy is—Emma Larke."

"Who is she?" asked Mr. Tanaka. "And why is it obvious?"

"Ah, she was dating Reese Dawkins," Sam Jackson answered. "But he broke up with her, and now she hates him and the Cogs. Emma wants to make Reese look bad," he argued. "What better way than to steal his signs and give them to Cody Howard? She doesn't want Reese to win the batting championship."

"We didn't know that Emma used to date Reese," said Jessie. "That gives her a motive."

"But it doesn't prove that she's the spy," said Violet softly.

"She might be the spy," said Winn, who was now serious. "But you have to consider Carlos, too."

"I like Carlos," said Mr. Tanaka. "He's a good worker and a cheerful person. Why in the world would he steal our signs?"

"I know why," said Winn.

"I know why, too." Sam Jackson said. "Carlos is a good ball player. He tried out for the team this past spring. Carlos wanted to be catcher. He was good... but just not good enough. We signed Reese Dawkins instead."

"I think it's Carlos," said Winn. "He wants to make Reese look bad so that the Cogs will accept him at the next tryout."

Benny spoke up. "Why does Carlos give you envelopes during the game?" he asked Winn.

"Envelopes?" asked Mr. Tanaka. "What envelopes?"

"The kid is crazy," said Winn. "Carlos doesn't give me any envelopes."

Jessie, Violet, and Henry all shook their heads. "Yes, he does," said Jessie. "We've all seen Carlos bring you hot dogs and soft drinks. And sometimes he pulls an envelope out of his pocket and hands it to you."

Mr. Tanaka looked at Winn. "What is this about?" he demanded. "You aren't taking money from the fans, are you? I pay you well, and you must never take money from the fans. Everything that Wheelie does must be free to the fans."

Winn nodded his head. "I can explain," he said. "I forgot about the envelopes. There's nothing in them but notes. They're notes from the fans."

"What kind of notes?" asked Mr. Tanaka.

"The fans write down ideas on what kind of stunts I should do," answered Wheelie. "Some of them want me to skip rope, for example. I can't do that, I'd trip and break my neck."

"Hmmm," said Mr. Tanaka, rubbing his chin. "It does not seem like a good idea."

Henry and Benny looked at each other. They knew that Wheelie asked for money when Henry had asked for an autograph.

"Should we say something?" Benny whispered to Henry.

Henry shook his head. Wheelie liked to joke a lot. Maybe Wheelie had been joking with him about the autograph. For all Henry knew, maybe Wheelie was telling the truth about the envelopes.

Mr. Tanaka looked at everybody in the room. "We all agree that somebody is stealing signs."

Everybody nodded.

"And we agree that we have no proof of who it is." Mr. Tanaka went on.

Everybody agreed.

"If the spy isn't discovered and stopped, the Cogs will not win the pennant this year."

CHAPTER 5

Back to the Bleachers

That night, Grandfather and the children ate dinner at the inn where they were staying. After dinner, the children talked in their room.

"Winn said the envelopes he gets don't have money in them," said Benny. "But Henry and I saw money fall out of an envelope in his pocket."

"Yes," added Henry. "There were lots of one-hundred dollar bills in the envelope. I don't think anybody would pay a hundred dollars for a Wheelie autograph."

"Me, neither!" shouted Benny.

"We didn't know that Reese Dawkins used to be Emma's boyfriend," said Jessie. "I think she wants him to fail at his job as catcher."

"We didn't know that Carlos wants to be the Cogs catcher," added Henry. "He also wants to see Reese fail."

"Mr. Tanaka was very upset when we mentioned Mr. X," said Violet. "I wonder why."

"Wheelie was making fun of us," said Benny. "It's not nice to make fun of people."

"You're right, Benny, it's not," said Jessie.

"Tomorrow is the third of the five games," Henry said. "Tomorrow we have to figure out which of our suspects is the spy."

* * * *

The next morning the children walked straight to the owner's office.

"We would like to help you again today," they told Mr. Tanaka.

"Thank you," he said, "but I think the best way you can help me is to find the spy. So

I would like you to spend all the time you need doing that. Where would you like to sit today?"

The Aldens had talked it over the night before. They told Mr. Tanaka that they needed to sit in the bleachers. He handed them tickets to the same four seats they'd had the first day.

"Before you go," said Mr. Tanaka, "there's something I must tell you."

The children waited.

Mr. Tanaka cleared his throat. "Yesterday I did not tell you something—something I should have told you. It is about the man you call Mr. X."

"What about him?" asked Violet, who could see that Mr. Tanaka was having trouble talking about this.

"Mr. X is really Simon Brock. Do you know who Simon Brock is?"

Henry, Jessie, Violet, and Benny all shook their heads.

"He's a famous movie producer," said Mr. Tanaka. "He grew up in Clayton. For three summers, he was batboy for the Clayton Cogs. Now he likes to come back each summer and watch the games. He's a big Cogs fan."

"We could tell that he likes the Cogs," said Henry. "But why did he want us to call him Mr. X?"

"Simon Brock doesn't want to be recognized," explained Mr. Tanaka. "He's afraid that if anybody knows who he is, they'll bother him. So many people want to be movie stars, they might not let Mr. Brock watch the game in peace."

Jessie nodded. "What is Mr. X—I mean, Mr. Brock—doing with a notebook and headphone?" she asked.

"Oh, that," laughed Mr. Tanaka. "He told me he's working on an idea for a new movie. Whenever he gets an idea, he writes it down. Or he records it by talking into his headphone."

"Wow!" said Benny. "He must be working on a baseball movie!"

Everybody looked at Benny. "Why do you say that?" asked Mr. Tanaka.

"Because every time something exciting

happens in the game, Mr. Tanaka takes out his notebook," said Benny. "Or he talks into his headphone."

"Hmmm," said Mr. Tanaka. "Well, if he is working on a movie, I hope he films it in Cogwheel Stadium."

* * * *

"We're down to three suspects," said Jessie. "Each of us should watch one person very closely."

"I'll watch Emma Larke," said Violet.

"I'll watch Wheelie," said Henry.

"And I'll watch Carlos Garcia," said Jessie.

"I'll watch the game," said Benny. "I want the Cogs to win!"

The others laughed. "*Somebody* has to watch the game," said Henry.

"It's an important job," said Benny. "Do you think we have time for some hot dogs before we begin work?"

"There's Carlos," said Jessie as Carlos walked toward them.

"Hello," said Carlos. "Ready for some red hots?" he asked.

"We're hungry," said Henry. "We'd like eight hot dogs."

"Good choice!" said Carlos with a smile. "If I remember right, all four of you like mustard." He topped their dogs with mustard and passed two hot dogs to each of the children.

"Do you think the Cogs will win today?" Jessie asked him.

Carlos no longer smiled. In fact, he looked very sad. "I don't think so," he said. "Every time Cody Howard comes to bat, Reese Dawkins calls the wrong pitch."

"Is it true that you tried out for the team?" asked Jessie.

"Who told you that?!" Carlos looked at them suspiciously.

"We heard Sam Jackson, the manager, say so," said Jessie.

"Oh," said Carlos. "Yes, it's true. The manager didn't pick me. But look at the bad job Reese is doing—I'll bet Sam Jackson picks me next year."

Carlos walked up the aisle to sell more hot

dogs. The Aldens ate their food.

A woman in tan pants and a light trench-coat sat down in front of them. She wore dark sunglasses and a big hat with a brim.

Violet thought they were strange clothes to wear on a hot summer day.

The woman turned around and said, "Hello to all of you."

Violet realized that the young woman was Emma Larke.

The Aldens said hello. Violet asked Emma if she thought the Cogs would win today.

"No," said Emma sadly. "I don't think so."

Violet didn't understand why Emma looked sad. Didn't Emma want the Cogs to lose?

Carlos returned and said hello to Emma. He sold her a hot dog. As he handed it to her, she whispered something to him. Carlos smiled.

Henry saw Wheelie coming down the aisle. Every few steps Wheelie did a little dance.

When he reached the Aldens, Wheelie sank to his knees. He clasped his hands together as if begging. He shook his head back and forth. Then Wheelie stood up and pointed a hand down toward Emma Larke's head. Wheelie nodded his head up and down. Wheelie was telling them that he thought Emma was the sign stealer.

Wheelie went to his special platform and sat down. Carlos brought him a hot dog and a soft drink.

"Yesterday Winn thought Carlos was the sign stealer," Henry told the others. "I wonder what made him change his mind?

The game began. When Reese Dawkins came to bat, Emma stood up and pointed at him. "You're history," she growled in a deep voice. "You're gone, Reese Dawkins. Gone!"

"Look," Benny whispered to Violet. "She's pointing with her left hand."

"Yes," said Violet. "I noticed that Emma is left-handed.

"Maybe she's the one who wrote Wheelie's name on that envelope," said Henry. He remembered the funny slanted handwriting.

Reese Dawkins hit a home run right at Emma. She ducked, and so did everybody else around her. Wheelie turned three cartwheels on his platform. The Cogs were leading, 1-0.

When Cody Howard came to bat, Emma stood again. She pulled her hat lower on her head and thrust out her arm. She pointed at Cody and growled, "Get the job done, Cody!"

Jessie watched Carlos, who stood staring at Cody Howard. Carlos banged the lid of his hot dog box three times.

Henry watched Wheelie, who was leaning back in his special chair. Wheelie looked like he was relaxing and wasn't worried.

Cody Howard smashed a triple and drove in one run.

"What if there are two sign stealers?" asked Jessie. "What if Carlos and Emma are a team?"

"Or Carlos and Wheelie," said Henry.

"What if we can't prove who it is?" said Violet.

The children looked at each other. They had promised Mr. Tanaka and Sam Jackson that they would discover who was stealing signs. What if they just couldn't find the proof?

The Cogs lost the game, 2-1.

The Aldens watched as the fans started to leave.

Violet noticed that Emma Larke did not look happy. But if Emma wanted the Hatters to win, shouldn't she be happy?

Jessie noticed that Carlos slumped down into an empty seat. He looked very sad.

Henry watched Wheelie walk away. It was impossible to see inside Wheelie's costume, to see if he was happy or sad.

CHAPTER 6

Mr. X Explains

At the top of the aisle, Henry and Jessie went in one direction. Violet and Benny went in the other. They hoped to find Mr. X before he left the ballpark.

But ten minutes later, neither group had found Mr. X.

"What should we do now?" asked Violet when they all met up again.

"Let's go outside," answered Jessie.

So they left the stadium, which was still crowded with fans. Unhappy fans, because

the Cogs had lost three games in a row to the Hatters. The Cogs *had* to win the last two games. If they didn't, they would lose the pennant race to the their biggest rival.

"There he is," said Benny. He pointed to a souvenir stand.

Mr. X stood there, holding three different kinds of Cogs baseball caps.

"Hello," said Jessie.

Mr. X turned. "Why, hello," he said.

"We need to talk to you about the sign stealing," said Henry.

"Sure," said Mr. X. He chose one of the hats and paid for it. "Let's step out of the crowd," he said. He led them to the shade of a tree.

"What made you decide that signs are being stolen?" Jessie asked him.

"That's easy," replied Mr. X. "It's clear to anybody who knows baseball well. Cody Howard knows which pitch is coming next. He waits for just the right pitch. Then he hits a triple or home run and the Hatters win the game." Mr. X looked at them closely. "Why are the four of you so interested?" he asked.

"We're working for Mr. Tanaka," Jessie explained.

"We told Mr. Tanaka we had three solid suspects," Jessie explained. "Plus one not-so-likely suspect."

"That was you," Henry added.

"*Me?!*" Mr. X said. "Why me?"

"Because you're always taking notes at the game," said Violet. "And then you speak into your headphone."

Mr. X smiled. He pulled out his notebook and wrote in it. Then he spoke into his headphone.

"New idea," he said. "Four kid detectives try to discover who's stealing signs."

Mr. X looked at the Aldens. "You all look trustworthy," he said, "so keep what I'm telling you a secret. My name is Simon Brock. I'm a movie producer."

Henry nodded. "We know," he said. "When we mentioned you as a suspect, Mr. Tanaka told us who you are."

"So," said Simon Brock, "I'm off the

suspect list because I'm a movie producer?"

Jessie shook her head. "No," she said. "You're off the suspect list because you can't see the catcher's signs. And Cody Howard can't see you when he's at bat."

Simon Brock laughed and spoke into his headphone. "The kid detectives are very smart," he said. "They solve the case." He smiled. "You're giving me great ideas for a new movie," he told them.

Henry nodded. "We just want to know why you think Emma Larke is stealing signs."

"Who?" asked Simon Brock.

"Emma Larke," said Violet. "Yesterday she was wearing a lavender dress. You pointed to her and said she was stealing signs."

"Right!" said Mr. Brock. "I didn't know her name. Yes," he said, "she's the one who's stealing signs."

"Why are you so sure?" Henry asked again.

"She's so easy to see," explained Mr. Brock. "She calls attention to herself. She wears very different clothing each day."

"Did you see Emma do anything today

that made you think she was stealing signs?" asked Violet.

Mr. Brock rubbed his jaw. "She did the same things she always does," he said. "She stands up when Cody Howard comes to bat. She shouts something. She waves her hat. Then Cody hits a home run or a triple. That might mean something, but I don't know what."

"Neither do we," confessed Henry. "We wanted to figure out who the spy was today. But we still have the same three suspects."

"Who are the other two?" asked Simon Brock.

"We don't want to say," Violet explained.

Mr. Brock nodded. "Spoken like true detectives," he said. Then he sat down on a bench. "This is serious stuff," he said. "The Cogs must win both of the last two games. If there's anything I can do to help you, just let me know."

* * * *

"Why so glum?" Grandfather asked at dinner.

"We haven't discovered who the spy is," explained Violet. "At today's game we watched all three very closely. But we couldn't tell which one was stealing signs."

"All three do things when Cody Howard is at bat," Henry explained. "Things that could be signals."

"We promised Mr. Tanaka we would help," said Jessie. "But we're getting nowhere."

"I'm sure that's not true," said Grandfather. "You are all very good thinkers. You must be getting somewhere."

"If we could just rule out one of them," said Henry. "Then we would be down to two suspects."

"But we still wouldn't know which of the two *is* the spy," argued Jessie.

"We can't guess," said Violet. "That wouldn't be fair."

"But if we had only two suspects, we could isolate one," said Henry.

"*I-so-late?*" asked Benny. "What does that mean?"

"Remember when you had the measles?"

Jessie asked Benny. "You had to stay home. Nobody could come visit you. You were *isolated* so that other people wouldn't catch the measles from you."

Benny looked confused. "Are we going to put a suspect where nobody can see him?" he asked.

Henry laughed. "Something like that," he said. "If we can down to two suspects, we can put one of them where Cody Howard can't see him."

"Yes!" said Jessie excitedly. "Let's make a list of all the clues after dinner. I'm sure if we think hard, we can figure out who is innocent."

"That would leave us with two suspects," said Violet.

"Let's make our list right away," said Benny, looking around. "Right after dessert, I mean."

CHAPTER 7

Who Is the Spy?

The children had the inn's game room all to themselves. They sat at one of the tables and Jessie pulled out her notebook.

"Do we all agree that Simon Brock isn't a suspect any more?" she asked.

Henry, Violet, and Benny nodded their heads. "He's just enjoying the baseball games," said Henry. "And thinking about movies."

"So," said Jessie, "let's begin with Carlos Garcia." She wrote his name in her notebook.

Then they discussed all the things that made it seem as if Carlos might be stealing signs. Jessie listed them.

Carlos Garcia

• Carlos dislikes Reese Dawkins, the Cogs catcher, and wants to replace him.

• Carlos hands Winn envelopes during the ballgame — maybe he and Winn are working together to steal signs.

• Carlos put an envelope into Emma's straw bag.

• Carlos and Emma talk about Reese Dawkins. They both want to see Reese Dawkins fail. Maybe Carlos and Emma are working together to steal signs.

• Carlos wears a pennant on his cap: he can be seen all the way across the ballpark.

• Every time Cody Howard comes to bat, Carlos bangs the lid of his vendor's box up and down. Could this be a signal to Cody?

"This looks bad," said Henry. "Carlos does a lot of suspicious things."

"We can't prove that Carlos is stealing signs," said Jessie. "And we can't prove that he's not stealing them."

"What about Emma Larke?" asked Benny.

Jessie made a new list.

Emma Larke

• She dislikes Reese Dawkins, the Cogs catcher, and wants to see him fail.

• She wears things that make it easy for the batter to see her.

• Whenever Cody Howard comes to bat, Emma stands up and shouts and waves her hat. This could be a signal to Cody.

• She was talking to Carlos Garcia about Reese Dawkins, the catcher.

• She received an envelope from Carlos Garcia.

"Emma is doing a lot of suspicious-looking things," said Violet.

"Maybe the things she's doing are *too* suspicious," said Henry.

"What do you mean?" asked Benny.

"Well," said Henry to his younger brother, "if you were stealing signs, wouldn't you try to hide it?"

Benny thought about this. "I would never steal," he said. "But a person who steals tries to hide it."

"Emma doesn't seem to hide what she's doing," said Violet.

"Let's go to our last suspect," said Henry.

"Winn Winchell," said Jessie as she wrote the name. "The team mascot."

"Also known as Wheelie," Benny said.

The others laughed.

The children spent a long time discussing Wheelie. Jessie wrote the list.

Wheelie
• Wheelie receives envelopes from Carlos during the game. Maybe Wheelie and Carlos are working together to steal signs.
• Wheelie has a very clear view of the catcher's signals.
• Wheelie makes motions each time Cody Howard is at bat. Sometimes he holds his nose, sometimes he holds both hands out to the side.
• Wheelie seems to want money. He seems

to want fans to pay for autographs.

• Benny and Henry saw an envelope with money in it fall out of Wheelie's pocket.

"This is a tough mystery to solve," Violet said. "All three people look guilty."

Henry stood up and paced around. "I wish we had been able to figure out who the spy was today."

"Me, too," said Benny. "But all three of them did the same things they always do."

"I am very sad," said Violet. "We don't have a name to give Mr. Tanaka tomorrow morning. That means the spy will continue spying. And that means the Cogs will lose tomorrow's game."

"But," said Henry, still walking back and forth, "I think we can tell who's *not* guilty."

Jessie nodded. "Yes. Who do you think is innocent, Benny?"

"Emma." said Benny. "Because she doesn't hide what she's doing."

"Very good," said Jessie with a smile.

"I think Emma is innocent, too" said Violet. "And I think I know why she wears different clothes. We can ask her tomorrow."

"Then we will have two suspects," said Jessie. "Carlos and Wheelie."

"We will *i-so-late* one of them," said Benny. "Like when I had the measles."

Henry sat back down. "This will be the most important decision we make," he said. "If we isolate the right person, nobody will be there to give stolen signs to Cody Howard."

"That means the Cogs will have a fair chance to win the game," said Jessie.

"We can think about this while we sleep," said Violet. "In the morning we can decide who to isolate."

The others agreed.

"There's one more thing we can do," said Jessie.

"What's that?" asked Henry.

"We can get two autographs. I'll get one, and Benny can get the other one."

"Good thinking," said Henry. "The autographs will help us."

CHAPTER 8

Emma's Clothes

The next morning the children went to Cogwheel Stadium with Grandfather. They arrived so early they had time to play in the ballpark outside the stadium. As soon as they saw cars arriving for the game, the Aldens put away their bats and balls.

Just inside Cogwheel Stadium, they waited for Emma Larke to show up. "I wonder what Emma will be wearing today?" said Benny.

They saw her coming through the turnstile. Today she was wearing a Cogs baseball cap, an orange Cogs baseball shirt, and white baseball pants.

"I thought Emma hated the Cogs," whispered Jessie.

"Emma looks very sad," said Violet.

Henry said hello and asked Emma if they could talk to her.

"Talk?" said Emma. "What about?"

Before Henry could start asking the questions they needed to ask, Benny blurted out, "Why are you wearing a Cogs uniform?"

Emma started to cry. "I'm a Cogs fan, really I am. I should have been rooting for them all along. And now," she said, crying harder, "the Cogs won't win the pennant. It's all my fault!"

"How is it your fault?" asked Jessie.

"I rooted for Cody Howard," said Emma, "just because I was so mad at Reese Dawkins! And look what happened—every time I cheered for Cody, he hit a home run! Or a triple! If only I hadn't cheered for him."

Emma wiped tears from her eyes. "It's all my fault," she repeated.

"It's not your fault," said Henry, "unless you were telling Cody which pitch was coming."

Emma stopped crying and looked at Henry. "Huh?" she said. "You mean like in sign stealing?"

"Yes," said Jessie, "that's what we mean."

Emma looked at the Aldens without saying anything. She seemed to be thinking. "Do you mean somebody is stealing signs and giving them to Cody?" she asked.

"Yes," said Henry, "that's what somebody is doing."

Suddenly Emma's eyes grew wide. "So you think I've been stealing signs?"

"Are you?" asked Jessie.

"No!" shouted Emma, who was now angry. "Why do you think it's me?"

"You wear a lot of different hats," said Benny. "And you wave them around when Cody comes to bat. Then he gets a big hit."

Emma became silent. The children waited

for her to speak, but she didn't say anything. Finally Henry asked, "Why do you stand up and wave your hat whenever Cody is at bat?"

"I want to explain," said Emma, "but I can't."

"Why not?" asked Henry.

"Because it involves another person," said Emma. "Somebody I shouldn't be talking about."

"That's okay," said Violet. "I know what you mean."

Emma stared at Violet. "You do?"

Violet smiled shyly. "Yes," she said. "The other person is Simon Brock."

All sadness vanished from Emma Larke's face. Her eyes lit up. She smiled happily. "Do the four of you *know* Simon Brock? I saw you *sitting right next to him* two games ago!"

"Yes, we know Mr. Brock," Jessie replied. "We know that he's a movie producer."

"Shhhh!" warned Emma, putting her finger to her lips. "Mr. Brock doesn't want anybody to know who he is. He wants to watch the games without being bothered."

"That's true," said Henry, "but how do you know that?"

"Oh," said Emma, twirling a lock of her hair around a finger, "I read film magazines all the time. I've seen photos of Simon Brock, so I recognized him in line one day. And," she said, "I could tell by how he dresses that he doesn't want people to know who he is. You know, the baseball cap pulled low, and the dark sunglasses."

"I know why you wear different clothes every day," Violet told Emma. "I know why you stand up and wave your hat."

Emma looked at Violet and smiled. "I believe you *do* know," she said.

"You want Mr. Brock to notice you," Violet said. "You want to be a movie star."

"Yes!" shouted Emma, clapping her hands together. "I want Simon Brock to see that I can act many different roles. One day I was an average fan. The next day I was a Southern lady. Yesterday I was a gangster! And today I'm a diehard Cogs fan."

Emma changed from happy to worried.

"Do you think that Mr. Brock has noticed me?" she asked.

"Yes," Henry answered. "He has definitely noticed you." Henry did not tell Emma that Simon Brock suspected her of being the sign stealer.

"Oh!" shouted Emma. "That's wonderful!" She became quiet and looked at Henry, Jessie, Violet, and Benny. "Do you think… do you think that you could introduce me to Mr. Brock?" she begged.

"Sure," said Jessie, "if you answer one question for us."

"Okay," Emma said. "What question?"

"We saw Carlos Garcia slip an envelope into your purse two days ago," Jessie explained. "What was in the envelope?"

Emma Larke blushed. "Oh, that," she said. "That was a note from Carlos asking me for a date."

"Thank you," said Henry. "We'll introduce you to Mr. Brock, but first we have a meeting with Mr. Tanaka."

* * * *

"Emma Larke looked guilty," said Jessie as the four of them walked to the owner's office. "But she *isn't* guilty. So now we're down to two suspects."

"But if Carlos wrote a letter asking Emma for a date, maybe he's innocent, too," said Violet.

"Maybe," Henry replied. "But remember that Carlos also gives envelopes to Wheelie. We don't know what's in those envelopes."

When the children entered Mr. Tanaka's office, they found him walking back and forth, back and forth.

"At last!" he said when he saw them. "Who's the spy?"

"It's not Simon Brock," Jessie told him. "And it's not Emma Larke."

"So," said Mr. Tanaka. "Is it Carlos Garcia? Or is it Wheelie?"

"We can't prove which of them is the spy," said Henry.

Mr. Tanaka sat in his chair and put his head in his hands. "Then it's all over," he moaned. "The Hatters will win."

Henry shook his head. "No. We have a plan to prove whether the spy is Carlos or Wheelie."

Mr. Tanaka looked up. "You do?" he asked, studying the children.

"Yes," said Jessie. "In order to prove which one is the spy, we have to separate them. We have to stop either Carlos or Wheelie from being where they can see the signs."

"And where Cody can see the spy," added Violet.

Mr. Tanaka thought about this a while. "It's a good plan," he said. "Which one should we take out of the bleachers?" he asked.

"We've talked about this," said Henry, "and we think Wheelie should leave the bleachers."

"Hmmm," said Mr. Tanaka, rubbing his chin. "I will invite Winn Winchell to sit with me in the owner's box today. In fact, I will *insist* that he sit with me."

"That's good," said Henry. "Do you have another person to play Wheelie?"

Mr. Tanaka looked at him. "Yes," he said,

"I certainly do."

"Good," said Jessie. "But if Cody Howard hits a home run the first time he comes to bat, you must act fast."

Mr. Tanaka nodded. "Excellent plan," he said. "If Cody hits a home run, then the spy is Carlos. I will have Carlos removed from the bleachers immediately, so that he won't be able to signal to Cody for the rest of the game."

Mr. Tanaka picked up his telephone and spoke to his assistant. "Have Winn Winchell come to my office," he said. "Immediately!"

In less than five minutes, Winn Winchell walked into the owner's office. As he walked in, the Aldens walked out.

CHAPTER 9

The World Looks Orange

Violet and Benny hurried to their seats in the bleachers. They sat behind Emma once again.

"Hi," said Emma, turning around. "Where are Henry and Jessie?"

"Jessie is getting an autograph," said Benny. "I'm going to get one, too."

"It's fun to get autographs," said Emma. "Whose autograph do you want?"

Benny looked all around. "I want Carlos's autograph," he said.

Emma laughed. "Carlos will be *thrilled* that you want his autograph, Benny!" She looked around. "Is Henry getting an autograph, too?"

"No," said Violet. "Henry is sitting in a different seat today."

"Oh," said Emma. "Well, I hope it's a good seat. I wouldn't want him to miss this game. The Cogs *must* win." She pounded the arms of her chair.

Violet and Benny looked all around, taking in the sights and smelling the hot dogs. Soon Jessie arrived.

"Got it!" she said, showing them a scorecard. Jessie tucked the scorecard into her pocket. "I'm hungry," she said, looking around. "And here comes Carlos."

Jessie bought hot dogs for Violet, Benny, and herself. She paid Carlos and gave him a tip.

"Thanks," said Carlos. "Where's Henry?"

"Oh, he's around here somewhere," said Jessie. She didn't want to say where he was.

Suddenly Benny jumped up. "It's Wheelie!"

he shouted, pointing down to the field. The big, fuzzy, orange mascot ran across the field, tossing rolled-up T-shirts to the fans.

"Wheelie!" shouted Benny. "Up here!"

Emma smiled at Benny. "I didn't know you liked Wheelie so much," she said.

"I love Wheelie," replied Benny.

Just then the mascot threw a rolled-up T-shirt toward their seats. The large cotton bundle came right at Emma. But Emma ducked at the last minute, and Benny caught the T-shirt.

All the fans applauded Benny. "Nice catch!" they shouted.

Benny was very excited. He unwrapped the T-shirt and held it up. Wheelie's picture was on the front.

"I'm going to ask Wheelie to autograph my shirt," said Benny.

Jessie and Violet smiled.

Emma frowned. "I don't know," she said. "Wheelie doesn't seem to like to autograph things."

Down on the field, Wheelie was jumping

up and down. He pumped both arms into the air. He spread his fingers in a *V* for victory. And then Wheelie did cartwheels all the way back to his special door.

The Cogs fans went wild. They applauded long and loud. "Go, Cogs, go!" they shouted. "Cogs will win! Cogs will win!" Of all the fans, Emma Larke shouted the loudest.

Benny kept looking back, to the top of the aisle. He waited for Wheelie. And then he saw the mascot at the top of the stairs.

Wheelie stopped to slap hands with fans. Whenever a fan handed him something to sign, Wheelie autographed it.

"Well, look at that," said Emma. "Wheelie is autographing everything!"

It took Wheelie a long time to reach the bottom of the aisle. Finally he reached the row where Jessie, Violet, and Benny were. He autographed Benny's T-shirt.

"Thank you," said Benny.

Carlos patted Wheelie on an orange shoulder. "Way to go, Wheelie. That's the right thing to do."

Wheelie climbed over the railing to his special platform and special seat.

The game began!

* * * *

From inside the mascot's costume, Henry thought the world looked orange. That was because one of Wheelie's orange eyelashes was drooping in front of the eye opening. Everything Henry saw from that eye looked a bit orange-y.

Mr. Tanaka had asked Henry to take Winn Winchell's place inside the mascot costume.

"But I've never been a mascot before," Henry had said. "I'm not sure I'd know what to do."

"You will do a great job," Mr. Tanaka had said. "And you will be helping the team."

So Henry had gone to Wheelie's dressing room and taken off his shirt and shoes. Just as he finished putting on the mascot's costume, there was a knock on the door.

Henry had opened the door. A boy about his age was there. He wore a Hatter's uniform. He handed Wheelie an envelope.

Henry took the envelope, but he didn't say anything. He knew Wheelie did not talk.

The boy turned and walked away quickly. Henry saw the words *Hatters Batboy* written across the back of the boy's uniform.

The envelope that Henry was holding was full of something papery. The handwriting on it said *Wheelie*. The handwriting slanted to the left! Henry put the envelope in one of the pockets of his shorts. Then he went out onto the field to throw T-shirts to the fans.

It's fun playing Wheelie, thought Henry, as he settled into his special chair.

The Cogs pitcher struck out the first Hatter, walked the second, and got the third to hit into a double play. In the bottom of the first inning, Reese Dawkins hit a home run with a runner on base. Henry stood up and did five cartwheels across the platform. Then he jumped up and down and pumped his arms in the air. The Cogs were leading, 2-0!

In the top of the second inning, Cody Howard was the first Hatter to bat.

Henry sat in the special chair. He put both feet flat on the platform. He crossed his arms and sat very, very still. Henry knew that if Cody Howard hit a home run, it meant that Carlos was stealing the signs.

Henry stared at Cody. It seemed like Cody Howard was staring right back at him! Of course Cody didn't know he was looking at Henry, since Henry was dressed as Wheelie. Cody hit a foul ball on the first pitch. He looked out toward the bleachers. He pointed his bat at the bleachers, then pounded it on home plate.

Henry heard a *clang-clang-clang* behind him. Carlos was banging the lid of his hot dog box up and down.

Now Henry realized what Carlos was doing. Carlos wanted to upset Cody Howard and make him miss! *Carlos is a true Cogs fan*, thought Henry.

Cody swung at the second pitch and missed.

The Cogs fans cheered loudly.

Cody stepped out of the batter's box and

walked around. Finally the umpire made him step back into the box. Cody pointed his bat toward the bleachers.

Henry did not move a muscle. He sat as still as a statue. He knew Cody wanted Wheelie to tell him what pitch was coming.

Cody swung and missed.

"You're out!" shouted the umpire. Cody walked back to the Hatters dugout. He glared toward the bleachers.

Carlos tapped Wheelie on the shoulder and handed him a hot dog and soft drink. "I love your new style, Wheelie! The fans love the jumps!" Carlos bent low so only Wheelie could hear him, "I'm glad to see you're signing autographs for free. That's what a mascot should do."

Henry nodded. He looked at his hot dog. *How am I going to eat this with a costume on?* he wondered.

The Cogs didn't score in the second or third innings. Neither did the Hatters. The score stood at 2-0. In the top of the fifth, Cody Howard came to bat again.

Once again Henry sat very still. His feet were flat on the platform. His arms were folded against his chest.

Once again Cody Howard seemed to be looking straight at him. Cody pointed his bat and pounded the plate. Henry could see Reese Dawkins hold down two fingers: curve ball. Henry watched the pitcher release the ball. He watched it zoom toward the plate, then curve. He saw Cody Howard swing and miss.

Cody pounded his bat on the plate. He pointed his bat at the bleachers. He scowled.

Wow, thought Henry. Cody is so angry that even if I signaled what pitch was coming, he would swing and miss.

Swing and miss is what Cody did. Strike two.

Cody tried to blast the next pitch out of the park — but his bat hit only air.

"You're out!" shouted the umpire.

Wheelie jumped up and down. He pumped his arms. The fans roared their approval.

"I love the Cogs!" shouted Emma Larke.

"Go, Cogs!" shouted Carlos. "Go for the pennant!"

"Yay, Cogs!" shouted Benny. "Yay, Wheelie!"

Cody Howard did not get a hit at all. The Cogs won the game, 4-0.

When Henry climbed back over the rail and stood in the aisles, he was mobbed by fans. Some wanted his autograph, which he gave. Others just wanted to pat him on the back.

Wheelie waited until all the fans had left. Then he and Jessie and Violet and Benny walked to the owner's box.

* * * *

Mr. Tanaka, Grandfather, and Winn Winchell all sat in the owner's box.

Jessie saw how happy Mr. Tanaka looked. Grandfather looked happy, too. Winn Winchell did not look happy.

"Henry!" said Mr. Tanaka, jumping up. "You were wonderful!" He helped Henry take off the top half of the Wheelie costume.

"I caught a Wheelie T-shirt!" said Benny,

pulling the shirt over his head. "And I got Wheelie's autograph, too," he said, pointing to where Henry had signed the shirt *Wheelie*.

"Yeah, yeah," growled Winn Winchell. "So the kids all had fun." He pointed at Henry and said, "But this kid can't play Wheelie like I can."

Winn jumped up and clenched his fists. "Tomorrow *I'm* the mascot again," he said.

"No," said Mr. Tanaka, "you're not."

"What?!" Winn shouted. "I'm the mascot! This kid isn't the mascot!"

"The Cogs won today," Mr. Tanaka said to Winn. "The Cogs and Hatters are tied for first place. Whoever wins tomorrow wins the pennant."

"What's that got to do with the mascot?" demanded Winn.

Mr. Tanaka pointed at a chair. "Sit down," he told Winn.

Winn glared at the owner, but finally Winn sat down.

"The Cogs have lost games they should have won," said Mr. Tanaka, his voice stern.

"The Cogs have lost because somebody was stealing signs."

"Stealing signs isn't a fair way to win," said Benny.

Winn waved his hand at them. "It's got nothing to do with me."

"Yes, it does," said Henry. "You're the sign stealer."

"You're crazy," answered Winn.

Henry reached into a pocket and pulled out an envelope. "Today the Hatters batboy came to Wheelie's dressing room. When I was in costume, he handed me this envelope."

"That's mine!" shouted Winn, jumping up.

But before Winn could grab the envelope, Mr. Tanaka stepped forward and took it from Henry's hand.

CHAPTER 10

The Spy Is Out

"Give me that!" shouted Winn. "It's mine!"

Mr. Tanaka ignored the shouts. He opened the envelope and pulled out what was inside.

"Money," said Mr. Tanaka. "One-hundred dollar bills." He counted the bills. "Ten of them!" Mr. Tanaka glared at Winn. "What is this money for?" he demanded.

"The money is from Carlos Garcia," said Winn. "Carlos wanted me to steal the signs and give them to Cody Howard. I refused."

"That's not true," said Benny.

"You don't know what you're talking about," growled Winn.

Henry spoke up. "The writing on the envelope isn't Carlos's handwriting."

"Yes, it is!" Winn insisted. "Carlos is the sign stealer."

"Mr. Tanaka," said Benny, "we can prove that isn't Carlos's handwriting." Benny reached into his pocket and pulled out a clean napkin. "Today I asked Carlos for his autograph. I watched him sign this napkin. This is his handwriting."

Mr. Tanaka held the envelope in one hand and the napkin in the other. "Carlos Garcia's handwriting does not match the handwriting on the envelope," he said.

Jessie spoke. "I also got an autograph today," she said, handing Mr. Tanaka a scorecard. "I asked Cody Howard to sign my scorecard," she said. "And he did."

Mr. Tanaka held the scorecard in one hand and the envelope in the other. "The handwriting is the same," he said.

"Okay, okay," said Winn Winchell. "So I was taking money from Cody. He wanted to win the batting title, and he was willing to pay me to help him."

"What you have done is dishonorable," said Mr. Tanaka. "You are fired," he added.

Mr. Tanaka opened the door. Four ballpark security guards stood in the hallway.

"Take Winn Winchell out of Cogwheel Stadium," said Mr. Tanaka. "Never let him come here again."

The guards escorted Winn Winchell out of the owner's box.

Mr. Tanaka waited until they were out of sight. Then he turned toward Henry, Jessie, Violet, and Benny. "Thank you so much for discovering who the spy was," he said. "And thank you also for all the other help you have given the Cogs and me."

"You're welcome," said Jessie. "We like to help."

"And we play fair," said Benny.

Mr. Tanaka smiled. "Tomorrow is the last game of the season," he said. "If the Hatters win, they will win the pennant. If the Cogs win, they will win the pennant. The game will be a fair game, with no sign stealing, thanks to the four of you."

"Do we get to watch the game?" asked Grandfather. "Or will we be in your office working on seating plans?" he teased his old friend.

"We will be sitting right here, in the owner's box," said Jim Tanaka. "And Jessie, Violet, and Benny will be with us."

Everybody looked at Henry.

"I know where I'll be," said Henry.

* * * *

The last game of the season was a night game. Grandfather couldn't park the car in his usual space because the stadium parking lot was so full.

"Are you adding more parking spaces for next year?" Violet asked him.

"Yes," said Grandfather. "And if the Cogs win the pennant tonight, I'll bet I have to add even *more* seats and parking spaces."

"I hope they win!" said Benny. He was

wearing his autographed Wheelie T-shirt.

Henry went to Wheelie's dressing room. Jessie, Violet, and Benny hurried to the owner's box with their grandfather.

The owner's box was above the ground seats of Cogwheel Stadium. It was just to one side of home plate.

"This is a great view," said Jessie, looking out at the ballpark through the open windows.

"Did we miss Henry?" asked Benny.

"Henry did a wonderful job as Wheelie," said Mr. Tanaka. "He gave away more T-shirts and water bottles than ever. Now he's on his way to the bleachers."

"Did he jump up and down and pump his arms?" asked Violet.

"Oh, yes," said Grandfather with a chuckle. "And the fans loved it."

"I think the players loved it, too," said Mr. Tanaka. "They think Wheelie brought them luck yesterday, so they're glad he's doing the same thing today."

A vendor came into the owner's box and set a large tray of hot dogs on a table.

"Please help yourselves," said Mr. Tanaka. Then the game began.

"You can see the whole ballpark from here," said Jessie.

"Yes, the owner's box has an excellent view," said Mr. Tanaka.

"You can see the whole stadium from the bleachers, too," said Benny.

Mr. Tanaka and Grandfather laughed. "Yes," admitted Mr. Tanaka, "you can."

Benny looked toward the bleachers and spotted Carlos Garcia. Benny waved, even though Carlos couldn't see him. Benny saw Wheelie sitting in his special chair on the platform. Benny waved. Wheelie waved back.

"There are so many interesting people in the bleachers," said Violet. She was looking at Emma Larke, who was wearing the same Cogs uniform she wore yesterday.

"Look!" said Violet. "That's Simon Brock sitting next to Emma Larke."

"It was very good of you children to introduce her to Mr. Brock," said Mr. Tanaka.

Violet watched Emma and Simon Brock.

They were talking to one another, and Mr. Brock was writing something in his notebook.

In the bottom of the second inning, Reese Dawkins hit a home run. The fans rose to their feet and clapped loudly. Wheelie turned five cartwheels in one direction, then five more in the opposite direction.

"Good," said Mr. Tanaka. "If Reese gets one more hit and Cody doesn't get any, Reese will win the batting title. And the car!"

Before he stepped into the dugout, Reese Dawkins waved toward the bleachers. Carlos Garcia waved back. So did Emma Larke. And so did Wheelie. The Cogs were leading, 1-0.

Even though Cody Howard didn't get a hit, the Hatters tied the score in the top of the ninth, 1-1.

In the bottom half of the ninth, the Cogs loaded the bases. There were two outs, and Reese Dawkins came to the plate.

Wheelie jumped up and down on his platform and pumped his arms. The fans jumped up and down and pumped their arms.

Reese Dawkins blasted the ball out of the stadium — a grand slam home run! The Cogs won the ball game, 5-1.

The Cogs won the pennant!

This time Wheelie did not turn cartwheels. This time, Wheelie did three backflips!

The players rushed out onto the field to celebrate. They lifted their caps toward the bleachers.

"Hmmm," said Mr. Tanaka. "I would be honored if you children would visit Cogwheel Stadium next year, too."

"I would love to see the Cogs play next year," said Jessie.

"I would love to catch another baseball," said Violet.

"And I would love to help Wheelie throw T-shirts and water bottles!" said Benny.

For a complete title list for The Boxcar Children® Mysteries,
please visit www.albertwhitman.com.